HAMER'S QUEST

a novel

JACK WALKER

Relax. Read. Repeat.

HAMER'S QUEST
By Jack Walker
Published by TouchPoint Press
Brookland, AR 72417
www.touchpointpress.com

ISBN-13: 978-1-952816-65-9

Editor: Kimberly Coghlan
Cover Design: Colbie Myles

Cover Images: Frank Hamer early1920s FBI photo (Wikimedia Commons); Waco Texas Ranger Museum: Texas Ranger Badge by Gary Todd (Flickr CC); Dramatic sunset just outside of Terlingua, TX by Dean Fikar (Shutterstock).

Visit the author's website at www.thetimeofyourlife24x7.com

First Edition

Printed in the United States of America

For Victoria, with all my love and respect

Author's Note

Hamer's Quest is historical fiction. Perhaps I should begin by apologizing for the use of "nigger" and other pejoratives used in this book. For a long time I was torn between using the abominable words or modern language. Reluctantly, because this novel is historical, I decided to use words as they were spoken in 1908-1911.

Some of the characters are historical figures. Frank Hamer, for example, may be the most famous Texas Ranger of all time. In the 1930s he tracked down Bonnie and Clyde. From 1908-1911 he was Marshall of Navasota, Texas. More than some of the actual events involving Frank have been dramatically embellished.

Many events—probably about 60% or so of the novel—are total fabrications and figments of the imaginary mind. The narrator, Jude McAbee, comes from deep within the caverns of my temporal lobe.

When he was 14-years-old Mance Lipscomb became Frank Hamer's wagon driver. In his 7th decade, Mance swept the campuses and the nation with his singing and fingerpicking guitar amalgam that blended blues, folk, country, and many other genres into a unique style. He played before 41,000 at the Berkeley Folk Festival in 1961, and packed arenas across the United States. His songs and style influenced Bob Dylan and many other influential performers. In his fading years, Mance recorded seven albums. Sadly, except for blues aficionados he is largely forgotten. For his vernacular and stories, I am indebted to the oral history of Mance Lipscomb nestled in the University of Texas, Austin library. Films and videos also helped. Some of his stories are fiction.

The hanging of John Campbell (dramatically embellished), and other hangings were true events. I transposed five atrocities from the 1920s and 30s back to 1908.

Christianity played a huge part in 1908 Texas society. I anticipate that modern Christians will accept with equanimity some of my tongue-in-cheek views on the denominations, especially the Presbyterians. The doctrine is entirely mine, but pretty close to 1908 John Wesley Methodism. I hope this historical novel will help you, dear reader, reflect on the ongoing Christian hypocrisy of our times.

White supremacy exposes the major theme of this novel. The Sherriff Scott incident was an actual even, for example. Sadly, white supremacy remains deeply ensconced in our society. I attempted to address some of the solutions to this malicious desecration, but my words fell disappointingly short of the target. I trust that you, dearest reader, will reflect on the words written here and create better solutions to restore love and peace for all.

"Jack Walker"
John Ingram Walker, MD
The Flying W Ranch
Lynn Grove, Texas

Prologue

JOHN CAMPBELL SAUNTERED down Washington Street on a splendid March afternoon. The Navasota landscape sparkled with sunshine. Bluebonnets and other wildflowers bloomed in the fields. Knee-high grass waved green on the prairies. The exhilarating freshness of freedom reminded John that all his days slaving in prison had been wasted and thrown away. This recurrent conviction filled his heart with bitterness and resentment.

He had been gambling with three white men in the cellar of Slim Cinderella's Bar, something that a smart nigga would never do, he told himself. If he lost, they would have all his money; if he won, they would rob him.

As certain as rivers flow to the sea, John's premonitions came true. A buffalo hunter named Ragsdale, with the body odor of a dead vulture, was drinking heavily. When John's three jacks beat his two pair, Ragsdale, enraged by the loss and inflamed by the alcohol, pulled a pistol, fired, and shattered a whiskey bottle sitting on the bar counter. John tackled the drunk, beating him with his fist. The other two gamblers subdued John, took his money, and sent for the sheriff.

At court, John pleaded self-defense. Ragsdale, bandaged across his broken nose and bruised cheek, fumed at John across the courtroom through the narrow slits of his swollen eyes. The all-white jury charged John with attempted murder and sent him to Huntsville State Prison for ten years.

While there, the white prison guards beat John unmercifully for minor infractions that John didn't know he had committed; sometimes they beat him for no other reason than their enjoyment. They put him in the hot box for five days when he protested the beatings. The white gun-bulls out in the fields lashed him if they thought he drank more water than allotted—or if his work pace slowed. When released, John swore revenge.

Navasota was a bad place to take umbrage against whites, but John was born and raised there. His Mama said to him, "This Navasota town is the meanest town in Texas. Mo' niggas kilt here than any place. They kill niggas just to have fun on Satiddy nights. If you try to hold up for your rights, they gonna get you for sure. Best you just shrink down like all of us here and don't rile 'em 'cause if you do you ain't goin' to last long. If you can't squeeze yo'self down, best to go on to someplace that you can find safety in."

John, whose imprisonment had made him meaner than a rabid dog, told his Mama, "I ain't gonna let no white folks throw this nigga out of my Navasota town. This is where I was born, and this is where I gonna stay. No man is gonna beat me down no mo'."

On that bright, sunny spring day, John, unencumbered by good sense and unspeakably aggrieved, strolled along the slat boardwalk of Washington Street. Ahead, he saw a colored man throw up his hands to ward off blows from his white master: "I didn' mean no hawm. Aw, please don't hit me no mo', Sir!"

John called out, "Nigga, why don't you hep yo'self? You just holdin' up yo hands and beggin.' Get up and defend yo'self!"

Robert Spurger, Mayor of Navasota, stood on the boardwalk with two companions, enjoying the fracas on the street. He turned to John. "You better mind your own bidness or I'll whip you down boy," he said.

John said, "You just try it. I don't think you can."

Spurger nodded to one of his companions, Pack Hardy, a stocky man with blacksmith arms and shoulders. Pack drew back and swung at John with an ax handle he had been carrying. John grabbed the ax handle, pulled a knife out of his belt, and sliced across Hardy's chest. Hardy, bleeding copiously from the wound, fell backward onto the boardwalk.

That day, Town Marshal W. B. Loftin, with the help of bystanders, wrestled John to the ground and put him behind bars. While he was in handcuffs, somebody yelled out that John ought to be lynched; then others yelled it too.

A bellowing and rowdy crowd surged toward the jail. Some of the men carried pitchforks; others had ax handles; a few held ropes. As the mob swarmed forward, townspeople frantically scampered out of the way, lest they get trampled.

Then, with a racket of ripping and smashing, the jailhouse door fell. A slim, tall man, Whip Wilson, demanded the cell key. Marshal Loftin refused to turn over the key at first, but when Whip pulled his Colt and thumbed back the hammer, he relented. Whip took the key and unlocked the jail cell, but John clung to the jail bars with such vigor and virility that four men couldn't pull him out.

John yelled, 'I ain't gonna come out an' give ya no chance to hang me. Ya come on, one by one, and I'll fight each one 'til all of y'all dead. Each of ya is a damn coward. The mob's only thang that make you strong. No one of ya brave enough to fight me alone."

A few of the enraged men in the mob pulled their guns and fired away. Then, the men celebrated, laughing and shouting, crowding around, guns going off like firecrackers. Blam-thud; blam-thud; blam-thud.

Nobody could say how many shots were fired—enough to cover most of John's body with holes. When the men grew tired of shooting, John looked like mincemeat pie. But that wasn't enough. One of the men—no one would say who—threw a rope around the neck of poor John, wrapped the end of the rope around the saddle horn, and drug him down the street all the way out of town and then back into town again.

Someone climbed up the iron stirrups on a telephone post. He hooked one end of the rope over a piece of iron at the highest point of the post and threw the other end of the rope down to the men on the ground who hoisted John up with the rope around his neck.

Mayor Spurger, arms crossed, watched the hanging while casually leaning against a porch column. As Whip walked toward him, Spurger turned with a menacing smile and seemed to glide through the swinging doors of Jimmy Lee's saloon.

Some newcomers riding into town saw John hanging from the telephone pole. They pulled their guns and shot him up again. John's riddled body looked like mush. He had no face. Blood ran out of the top of his boots. He hung there all night.

Early the next morning, when the sun was just beginning to pink the eastern sky, Miss Gladys Shine took a buggy ride, enjoying the cool morning air before the day became blazing hot. Miss Shine was the only daughter of Peter Welsh Shine who had made his money in railroad investments. Regular citizens considered twelve families in Navasota aristocratic. The Shine family was one of those twelve. With his considerable political power, Mr. Shine had helped Thomas Mitchell Campbell become governor of Texas.

Miss Shine adored her mare Buttercup, a magnificent high-stepping Hackney, a breed considered the world's most spectacular harness horse. The chestnut trotter, trained by Alexander Cassatt in Lexington, Kentucky, was pliant as a willow stem—and as gentle as a summer breeze. No one was awake when Miss Shine attached Buttercup to her Stanhope buggy. She decided to take a predawn ride through the empty Navasota streets.

On the outskirts of town, Buttercup, without warning wheeled around, canted the buggy on the left wheel, and spilled Miss Shine onto the ground, unhurt. Buttercup raced back to the barn, dragging the overturned buggy behind.

Miss Shine screamed, "What's wrong with my horse? She's a good horse. A tame horse. A trained pace horse."

The only other person on the street was Eddy Watson, a colored man, walking to milk cows at Mr. Brown's dairy barn. Hearing Miss Shine's cries, he called out to her, "I tell you what's the matter with that hawse. Look up at that man hangin' from that post, drippin' blood. That hawse smell that blood and took off."

Miss Shine looked up and swooned at the gruesome sight of John's body. She crumpled onto the ground.

When Buttercup fled up the barn road noisily, dragging an empty buggy, Mr. Peter Welsh Shine awoke and, naturally alarmed, followed the buggy marks. He soon caught up with his frightened daughter scurrying home. With much fanfare, Miss Shine downed an early morning glass of brandy and fell into her bed.

The next day, refreshed and inspired, she wrote a letter to Governor Campbell:

Dear Governor,

I am the daughter of Peter Welsh Shine. We met at the Governor's Ball. As I told you then, my family is so proud to have you as the new Texas governor because of your strong support of law and order. I am writing to you because our little town of Navasota is suffering from disorder.

Now Governor, I know that as a loyal Democrat, you favor the white man's vote. My family and I do too. The white man's vote, however, has gone too far in Navasota. This morning I came across the most awful sight. A black man was hanging from a telephone post. He was riddled with bullets. Blood was dripping into his boots. The bleeding body spooked my horse. She turned for the barn and spilled me into the street. I am doing fine now, but the town of Navasota is not fine.

Evil pervades Navasota. Everyday white men

abuse Negroes. They hit them. They beat them. They whip them. They shoot them. They kill them just for the fun of it.

Please send a Texas Ranger to clean up this town and stop the killing. Two rangers would be even better. Please send as many Rangers as you can spare. Many of the people here are vicious, cruel, remorseless, barbaric, and fiendish. Navasota has turned into a Texas Sodom and Gomorrah. Please send help quickly before God destroys Navasota with fire from above.

I am enclosing a modest twenty-five-dollar check to support your marvelous projects. I am certain Daddy will be sending more from time to time.

With all my support and warm regards,
I remain,
Miss Gladys Shine
Daughter of Peter Welsh Shine

Chapter 1

LIKE MY FATHER, I was a Methodist circuit rider. My father, Albert O. McAbee, who had an ironic nature, named me John Calvin McAbee. After he read the Apocrypha, he started calling me Jude. The name stuck. Growing up in Texas teaches cowboy ways—riding, roping, roundups, and rodeos. You also learn how to shoot to kill and how to survive when alone. My mother expanded my knowledge beyond cowboying, reading, writing, and arithmetic. She introduced me to Shakespeare, Greek mythology, and made me learn Latin, her favorite subject.

With my Stetson, jeans, and boots, I was as out of place as a mule at the Kentucky Derby when I enrolled at Yale Divinity School. No matter, I absorbed Greek, Hebrew, and theology just as well as the cultured and refined. Those Yankees loved theology more than they loved Jesus. Scholarship without spirit, I learned, was about as useful as a milk cow with no teats. I was eager to get back west where I could broaden my soul with Texas stretching out before me.

For several years, I moved from town to town preaching and praying and baptizing. Not sprinkling like my Methodist father, but baptizing like a Baptist wherever I could find a river or a pond deep enough for a good dunking. I felt the Lord's calling until I shot a Catholic priest for sodomizing a six-year-old boy. After that, I lost my zeal for preaching.

Every little Texas cow town needs two things: a preacher and a sheriff. I became a sheriff. Instead of preaching the book of the law, I moved from town to town upholding it, most of the time. Like snow on the windy Texas plains, I drifted.

Then I began to enjoy the spirit found in bottles. I liked spirited women even better. And I liked reading all kind of books. Books saved me from too much rowdy drinking and made me popular with the barmaids and such when I read to them.

Between sheriff jobs, I rode shotgun beside the driver on the Charles Bain Stage Line, taking the 600-mile trip from San Antonio to El Paso and back again. For a while, I joined Tom Horn as a bounty hunter until he shot a 14-year old boy. Tom said it was an accident, but they hanged him anyway. I figured a bounty hunter was just about as bad as the bounty I hunted and gave it up.

I went up to Colorado to pan for gold, but too much work for too little gain discouraged me quick. I made some money gambling until I fired my shaking pistol at a bottom-dealing cheater. Missed the charlatan but killed the mayor. I was sheriff at the time. Being a sheriff doesn't protect you from being hung, especially if the judge is the mayor's brother. So I skedaddled right quick, not giving them time to build a scaffold.

I made my way to Fort Worth to take a look-see at Texas Jack's Wild West Show and Circus. The show had a reenactment of the 1893 Shanghai Patrol where 3,000 Rhodesian warriors wiped out a 34-soldier unit of the British South Africa Company. Texas Jack played the lone survivor. Now that play seemed sort of silly to me. Why do a show on British people getting killed? I mean what about the Alamo or Adobe Walls? Anyway, there was plenty of fake blood and hand-to-hand combat and soldiers screaming and dying, so the people seemed to enjoy it.

A young man named Will Rogers did a few rope tricks in the show. I went backstage to talk to him. We got along fine. He told me he was going down to Argentina to work as a gaucho and asked me to go along. I thanked him but told him there were too many places in Texas that I hadn't seen that I wanted to see. If I had known Will Rogers would be famous in a few more years, I might have gone.

By and by, I heard there was trouble down in Terlingua. I like trouble. Keeps my energy up. Keeps things interesting. And ... where there is trouble, there is always work for someone who can handle a gun. So I studied up on the Terlingua problem.

For thirty years, the Mexican dictator Porfirio Diaz ruled with an iron hand. In 1906, anarchists lead by Ricardo Flores rebelled. His rebels raided villages that supported Diaz. They gunned down those who resisted or ran. They whipped and beat the unruly. They raped the women.

The raids didn't last long. The Mexican army ruthlessly suppressed the insurgents. The infantry rounded some of the rebels into a barn, barred the doors, and burned the barn down; other rebels were hanged with barbed wire; some were lined up against a wall and shot.

Flores got the message that rebellion wasn't a good idea and fled with Mexican forces in pursuit. He swam across the Rio Grande and sought sanctuary in Terlingua. Diaz demanded his arrest and extradition to Mexico.

Terlingua was a dusty border town made wealthy by Howard E. Perry, who owned the quicksilver mine. Mostly Mexicans worked in the mine. Perry installed the Chinos Hotel and free housing for the mineworkers. People crossed back and forth between Texas and Mexico. Smugglers and rustlers abounded.

The local lawmen were inexperienced and incompetent. For the most part, they could keep the bordellos peaceful and handle drunks and disruptive punks in the saloons and gambling houses, but they avoided gunslingers and hardcore fighters. The Rangers handled what the local law couldn't—the killers, desperados, rumrunners, rustlers—and they were often called to protect the border.

I decided to go down there to see what I could see.

Chapter 2

AS I RODE TOWARD Terlingua, the boundless blue sky filled my heart with wonder. The Davis Mountains provided a jumble of peaks alternating with lushly green undulating grassland that heaved and swelled. Rolling elevations and depressions stretched as far as the eye could see. The spring weather gave birth to wild flowers of all colors growing in the rocky land.

Several miles south of Alpine, the landscape became flat and ugly. Creosote bushes, a variety of prickly agave, yucca, mesquite, and fire-barrel cactus and other cacti filled the desert floor. Near Terlingua, I could make out the majestic peaks of the Big Bend Country.

A recent shower turned the narrow road into mud. A hog prodigious with fat wallowed in a muddy ditch, grunting and rooting. In the barrio, flat adobe shacks, some with rotting uncovered porches, gave the impression of small boats slowly sinking into a sandy sea. A few chickens pecked around in grassless dirt. A little garden fenced with chicken wire grew jimson weeds and dandelions. Pieces of bottles and rags and whatnots were scattered all around. Old crumpled papers blew across the hardpan yards. A rusty plow sat slapdash by the side of the road.

A young Mexican woman sat on a porch rocking monotonously back and forth, back and forth. Occasionally, she spat into an old tin can. She wore a tattered calico dress, filthy with brown stains and what looked to be dried up blotches of food. Her dull, flat eyes reflected a faraway, distant place as she cackled and sang to something unseen. At a crossroad, an hombre stood, talking to a señorita sitting in a wagon.

I rode Warrior up to the Sediento Saloon and reined in, dismounted, tied Warrior to the hitching post, and grabbed my shotgun out of the saddle scabbard. I never go anywhere without my takedown.

Sediento—I knew it to mean "thirsty" in Spanish. I was thirsty, sure enough, but I never got to the bar. As soon as I walked through those swinging doors, a Mexican wearing a serape fell at my feet. I jumped away. A tall man wearing dungarees and a tan vest over a blue shirt was kicking him. I could clearly see the Texas Ranger badge pinned to the big man's vest.

The Mexican struggled to stand, teetered toward the middle of the saloon, and turned. His stringy hair was filthy with grime. He had a wide scar running diagonally from his upper lip to just below his right eye. His serape was splattered with mud—or caked blood, perhaps. His canvas pants were tucked into his muddy boots. He pushed back the serape on the right side to expose a wooden-handled Colt.

"I'm not going back to Mexico," he said.

"The law says you are," the Ranger said, slow and deliberate. Three men turned from the bar. Keeping his eyes on the Mexican, the Ranger turned slightly so he could see the men behind him in his peripheral vision.

"They will torture me," the Mexican said.

"You reap what you sow. An eye for an eye," the Ranger replied.

A short man with the belly of a sow whispered in a voice so low, I could barely hear him. "Stay put, Ricardo."

The man next to him growled, "Kill him Flores."

A tall man unfastened his holster strap, and with his hand resting on his revolver, he moved away from the bar. He said nothing.

Flores crouched slightly and looked at the men behind the Ranger. They all had their hands on their guns. I pointed my 12-gauge at the three desperados. The men spread out a little. I racked the 12-gauge. Ka-chung. No one spoke. All was still and quiet. It was like a hot and dry October day when you can feel a Blue Norther coming from the distant plains long before it arrives.

Ricardo Flores took a breath and said, "I'm not going back." Then, he went for his gun.

With a deliberation that seemed to slow time, the Ranger drew his Colt, thumbed back the hammer, steadied the pistol, and shot Ricardo in the center of his chest. Ricardo catapulted backward before his gun was completely out of the holster. The Ranger turned and aimed his Colt in the direction of Ricardo's supporters.

Time wavered. A summer cloud blown by the wind dimmed the sun, darkening the room. The tall man who had unfastened his holster strap hesitated. His right hand on the butt of his Smith & Wesson trembled ever so slightly. Then he dropped his arm to his side, turned, and skedaddled out of the saloon. The other two followed.

The Ranger exchanged the spent shell from the .45-cylinder with a new one. He returned the Colt to its holster. He looked down at Flores. As he turned to walk toward a table at the back of the bar, he tipped his hat, and with an off-kilter smile, he nodded for me to join him. The ranger moved with effortless grace belying his size: 6'2" or 3"—around 200 pounds with massive shoulders and forearms forged at his father's blacksmith shop.

"You've got to be Frank Hamer," I said extending my hand and introducing myself. "I've heard all about you."

Frank returned my firm grip. We sat down. Frank took a seat with his back to the wall. I sat to his right. I could see the bar and look outside through the windows.

I ordered a Jack Daniel's, double, and was startled when "the strongest, roughest, toughest, cruelest Texas Ranger of them all, past and present," I had read about asked for a lemonade.

When the drinks came, I gave a toast, "To hard kicks and fast guns," I said.

Frank clinked my glass, but I could tell he didn't much care for my bravado. He had a hard, angular face with a prominent chin. His eyebrows were drawn almost together giving him a look of habitual alertness.

I took a couple of gulps from my whiskey, leaned back, and relaxed some as we began to get to know each other. Frank's courteous and gentlemanly bearing, the opposite from his wrath just a few minutes ago, dazzled me. I thought of a rattlesnake, calm and peaceful in the sun, ready to strike suddenly when threatened. But the man sitting across from me was no rattlesnake. He was friendly and warm, easy to talk to. When he gracefully dodged personal questions and guided the conversation back to me, I realized why. I was doing all the talking. Tolerably soon, he had learned pretty much all about me.

"You have a .45 Colt strapped to your side. Can you shoot it?" Frank asked.

"Might be able to hit a barn if it's big enough," I said.

"A regular sharp shooter. Annie Oakley must be quaking in her boots."

"Couldn't hit an outhouse though."

I told Frank about my preaching days and how killing that sodomizing priest caused some religious consternation—and ruined my aim with a pistol.

"Don't much need a pistol when you got a 20-inch 12-guage shotgun," Frank said.

"I call this attention-getter my takedown. I'm really good with my takedown. It's awful hard to miss with buckshot spraying all over a room."

"A Winchester shotgun with a 20-inch barrel gives you instantaneous respect in every saloon in every town in Texas," Frank said.

"This takedown converts more sinners than a dozen circuit-riding preachers," I said.

"Next time you want to kill a sodomizing priest, just show him your shotgun. He'll die of fright," Frank said.

A black hearse pulled by four mules had stopped outside of the saloon. A man with a narrow face and pen-point pupils climbed down and walked into the saloon. He wore a black long coat over black pants. The Edwardian coat made his pale skin luminescent with a deathly pallor. He grabbed the corpse by the arms and drug the body outside. A couple of bystanders helped him put Flores in the back of the hearse. He drove off without a word. I figured he was taking opium and needed to get back to his source.

Frank rolled up a cigarette. He took a puff and blew smoke rings toward the ceiling. We sat there, Frank puffing smoke loops, me sipping on my whiskey. Outside, the setting sun cast long shadows. The buildings and storefront had a sort of golden glow. Frank had a distracted, dreamy look as if he was seeing the future instead of the room unfolding before him.

After he finished his cigarette, Frank said, "Got some trouble in Navasota. Seems a big landowner by the name of Robert Spurger has been stirring things up. He has a gang of ruffians backing him. Need a deputy. You want to join up?"

"Is it dangerous?" I asked

"Not any more than going down Niagara in a barrel," he said.

"Sign me up," I said.

And that's how I became Frank's deputy. I like danger, I guess. Or at least I dislike boredom so much that I'll take danger over that. Danger might make you age faster or take your life before you expect it, but at least you're alive while you're living.

Chapter 3

FRANK AND I BOARDED the train in Alpine. When we reached Austin, we planned to get our horses out of the stock car and ride on to Navasota. At Langtry, the train stopped to resupply water for the steam engine. A young man boarded. He took a seat next to us. Despite his baby face, his perceptive brown eyes gave him an intelligent look. He wore a Stetson with a telescope crease, a blue bandana, red bib shirt, and dungarees. He had a strapped-on Colt and held a Winchester '73 in the crook of his left arm. His boots were deeply scratched.

"Howdy," he said. "I'm Monty Motes from Langtry, headed for Austin to join up with the Texas Rangers. I seen your badges. Why don't y'all deputize me and save me the trip? I got this here letter from Judge Roy Bean his self recommending me."

He showed us a scrawled-out letter signed by Judge Roy Bean with "The Law West of the Pecos and Langtry, Texas" rubberstamped.

> This here boy Monty Motes by name caught rustlers up at Pandale and brought them to me to hang. He also caught up with a horse thief that nobody else could find. He wants to be a Texas Ranger and I see no reason why not.

Sincerely,
Judge Roy Bean
The Law West of the Pecos
Langtry, Texas

Frank said, "We don't deputize people just because they have a Colt and a Winchester. Outlaws have the same. You look intelligent enough, but I've known a few outlaws that weren't too dumb."

I had planned to read on the train ride, but Henry David Thoreau's *Walden* suddenly bored me. I said, "Tell us about yourself."

He started up and began rattling on like a runaway train, hardly stopping for breath. His North Texas twang, poor grammar, his Huckleberry way of talking, and his enthusiasm for everything but a dead skunk caused us to sit back and listen.

"I was borned on the Charles Goodnight ranch way up in the North Texas panhandle. It's so far from everythin' and when that whistlin' winter wind, colder than a frosted frog, comes blowin' ice and snow, you think you're closer to the Arctic Circle than to Abilene. Mr. Goodnight called his ranch the JA Ranch on account that John Adair pitched in some money for bunkhouses, supplies, stock and such, but everybody knowed it was Mr. Goodnight's ranch in all but name. My dad he was one of the head wranglers on that ranch, and I followed after him whenever I could. At night around the campfire, if he was in the right mood, Mr. Goodnight would tell us about his adventures. He told us a bunch of plum good stories."

Sitting in first class has advantages. The porter came by. I ordered my favorite. This time, I wasn't surprised when Frank ordered lemonade. Monty asked for a Dr. Pepper. I was puzzled. I had never heard of the drink before. I gave Monty a bewildered look.

"Made in Waco," he said. "Named after the father of his girlfriend. Every time I drink a Dr. Pepper, I wonder how could a good drink like this come out of whistle-stop Waco."

I took a sip of Jack Daniel's whiskey. "Every time I drink Old #7, I think of beautiful women," I said toasting my glass to the sky.

"Ain't seen none in the Panhandle. All that wind and weather wrinkles them like prunes," Monty said.

"Heard the women in Austin are hot enough to sizzle your spurs," I said. "They dazzled one man's eyes so much that—WHOMP—they fell out of the sockets. Has been on his knees feeling around for them for more than a year now."

Monty laughed and looked out the window. After a little while, he looked at me and began talking in a somber voice. "One night, Mr. Goodnight up and told us about how his best friend Oliver Loving got shot in the arm by the Comanche and died of gangrene."

The train slowed and came to a stop. I looked out the window. Sheep were crossing the track.

Monty hunched forward in his seat and continued: "It was such a sad story the way Mr. Goodnight told it, his voice crackin.' Mr. Goodnight was such a strong, tough man, and to see him with tears in his eyes and hear a lump in his throat ... well I never ... it just goes to show the heart Mr. Goodnight had for his friend."

"You ride with a friend, your heart dies with a friend," I said.

By and by, the train started up again. We sat there for a while watching the landscape roll by. I was thinking about friends and loved ones I had lost. I wish they could be with me—in person—again. In a way, they never left. Their spirit rests in my soul. Their spirit is a part of me ... but I still miss the alive part.

The three of us got up, stretched, and headed for the lounge car where we sat down in cushioned chairs. I enjoyed another Jack Daniel's that was getting smoother with each swig. Frank, God bless him, ordered another lemonade. Monty who couldn't sit still very long without talking, started up again.

"I never know'd my real mama as she died givin' me birth. They say that my mama was so nice and sweet that everybody was mopey and sad. Most of the people was crying. And then Mrs. Goodnight stood up straight and said, 'Heck fire we don't go waterin' dead flowers when we got blossoms bloomin'' and she started raisin' me and teachin' me like I was her own child as she had none borned to her. And Mr. Goodnight he said 'the best way to handle death is to saddle up and ride away from it.'

"They say my dad took long rides up and down the canyon for weeks on end and still had sadness in him. I guess he found out what other people knowed that no matter how far you rode the burr in the saddle would always be there."

The train began to slow as it wound down into a canyon. The conductor got our attention: "Ladies and Gentleman. I'm sorry, *gentlemen*. There ain't no women on this trip."

"There ain't no gentlemen neither," someone yelled out.

Monty laughed. He had a contagious, robust laugh.

"Gentlemen," the conductor began again. "We are now crossing the Pecos Viaduct. When it was completed in 1892, it had the distinction of being the highest bridge in the United States and at 322 feet 10 ¾ inches in height, the third highest bridge in the world."

"How does its height rank now in 1908?" a young man asked.

"Hell, I don't know son. I'm just telling you what they wrote up for me to say," the conductor said. "If you are a Texan, tell others that this viaduct is the tallest bridge in the world until someone doubts you. Then you can argue about it."

"How did they build this thing across the canyon walls?" a man dressed in a business suit who looked like an accountant or banker asked.

"Section by section, my friend. Section by section," the conductor replied. "You can see pictures of construction in the smoking section of this train. You can look out the windows and see the Pecos River way below. If you stick your head out the window far enough and crane your necks, you can see from one end of the viaduct to the other. Be cautious about how far you lean though. We had a man tumble out the window the other day. He was a slim man. As he fell, we could hear him say, 'I'm all right so far.' They say he was an optimist."

A nervous chuckle permeated the lounge car, sprinkled in with a few groans from the more sophisticated passengers.

"Anyway," the conductor continued. "Using a daily work crew that averaged 67 people, the bridge was completed in just 103 days at a cost of $250,108. The completed viaduct is 2,180 feet long. The ironwork alone weighs 1,820 tons."

As the conductor talked, we all looked out the window at the impressive sight of lattice-like ironworks cantilevered from section to section across the canyon space, supporting the tracks and the heavy train. This massive structure didn't look stable to me. I figured a puff of wind could blow it over at any minute. I was mighty glad when the train made it across. I imagine most everybody else was too.

My heart was pumping fast, and my palms were sweaty. How could gunplay have little effect on my nerves while a railroad-bridge crossing causes a panicky feeling? Probably has something to do with experience or control. The more you do something, the less anxious you feel, but this can be a disadvantage too. A gunfighter who isn't alert and edgy won't live to fight again. As for bridges, I'd rather not get on that viaduct again, no matter how much experience I would gain.

As I was thinking these things, Monty began to talk again. I welcomed it. Soothed my nerves down.

"I learned a lot watching Mr. Goodnight. He is a powerful man. He won't back down to no one, but he will cheat no man, woman or child and the Indians neither. But he will hang rustlers and horse thieves faster than a rattlesnake can strike. Living with Mr. Goodnight made me want to be like him. He insisted on honesty and trustworthiness. He expected everyone to do the right thing. From then on, I determined to become a law and order man. There's a right and there's a wrong. Every one of us must face the consequences when we cross the line."

The train began to slow as we came into San Antonio. The conductor announced that we would stop in San Antonio for thirty minutes—enough time to get passengers off and reload others. We would unhitch a few of the fright cars and add some more. He encouraged us through-riders to stay on the train. We got up and walked around in the car but didn't disembark. There was a lot of jostling going on: the train moving up and moving back to hitch and unhitch the freight cars.

When the train started up, Monty kept on talking. I had never heard a man talk so fast and say so much. Monty's rat-a-tat way of speaking reminded me of a runaway buggy on a downside hill.

"By and by I got hunkering for adventure and told Mr. and Mrs. Goodnight so. Mrs. Goodnight teared up and said she didn't want her boy tilting with no windmills and asked me wouldn't I reconsider. She said my grammar was still bad and needed some workin.' Mr. Goodnight spoke up and said it was time for me to sow my wild oats and learn some things about survivin' on my own. Good grammar might get me into Harvard, he says, but I would have no common sense when I got out. Besides, he says, knowin' how to fend for yourself could make you rich in Texas. So Mrs. Goodnight dried her eyes, and said that the ranch would always be my home and come back from time to time and don't forget to write."

I glanced at Frank who stretched out in his seat with his left arm draped over the chair arm. He seemed to be enjoying Monty's palaver.

"I had heard about Judge Roy Bean and figured he had adventures to give, and sure enough, as soon as I got there, he give it. I caught an outlaw by waitin' at a water hole where he was sure to go. A few weeks later, I rounded up two horse thieves and marched them fifty mile though Val Verde County to Langtry. The Judge was real happy when I brought those horse thieves to him, and he didn't waste no time hangin' 'em. He banged his gavel, and then he strung 'em up," Monty said nodding his head in wonderment.

"That's the law in the Trans Pecos," Frank said with an appreciative nod.

"After I'd been in Langtry for a while waiting for more outlaws to chase down, Judge Bean told me there was no adventure like a Texas Ranger adventure. I got real excited to try it out so he wrote me this letter, and here I am," Monty said with anticipation in his voice. "Well what do you think? Can you sign me up to be a Texas Ranger?"

Frank who had been smiling all the while Monty was talking said, "Well ... you sure can tell a good story ... but that's not my decision to make. From the sight of you, I think you'd make a good Ranger, but looking is different from doing. I'll tell you what; when we get into Austin, you just ride up to the Capital to see Captain John H. Rogers of the Texas Rangers. Give him this note by way of introduction."

Frank asked the porter to bring him some writing material. When he got it, he scribbled out a note. I didn't get to see what he wrote exactly, but I could tell by the expression on Monty's face as he read it that the note was of the positive kind.

"Captain Rogers is rawhide tough. He'll test you out," Frank said. "He'll have you ride the territory with some Ranger somewhere who will size you up. If you're as good at doing as you are at talking, I imagine you'll get that badge."

Monty sat back in his seat, a look of anticipation on his face. For the first time we met him, he had nothing to say. We sat in silence the rest of the way to Austin, and I was mighty glad of it.

Chapter 4

WHEN WE FINALLY departed the train in Austin, the noises, smells, and sights overwhelmed us. I heard carriages rattling, wagons rumbling, steam hissing, trains whistling, heels tapping, the clip-clop of hooves, the rising and falling of conversations, the cries of vendors, and an earsplitting cacophony of automobile sounds.

"What's that smell?" Monty asked wrinkling his nose.

"Bunch of things mixed together," I said. "I smell horse manure. Burnt oil, for sure. Gasoline fumes. Food cooking."

"City stink," Frank said.

"These women sure don't stink," Monty said. "They fill out their clothes right well. Looky at that one. Ankle showin'. Sassy lookin' women."

"Colorful hats," I said.

"Anyone looking at hats is misusing his eyes," Monty said.

"I don't like looking at things I'll never have," I said.

Just then an automobile passed by belching oil, fire, and smoke. "That's something I'll never have and something I'll never want," Frank said with disgust.

"Loud ... smelly ... ugly," Monty said. "A rattletrap of noise and stink."

"Looks like it could fall apart anytime," I said. "Fall apart or burn down."

"Or poison us all to death with those fumes," Monty said.

"Progress ain't all that it's told to be," Frank said.

"Don't worry," Monty said. "Just a fad. Them cars will all be gone in a year's time."

"Don't count on it," Frank said.

"Let's ride around and take in the sights," I said. "I read that over 35,000 people live in Austin."

"That's way more than lives in all of the panhandle," Monty said.

"And there's way more to see that we've never seen," I said.

"I've read about these things. But seeing is different from reading," Frank said.

"Seeing is knowing. Reading is wanting to see," I said.

"I guess readin' makes you two highfaluting scholars," Monty said.

"Scholars and gentlemen," I said.

"If you read books, you are scholars in my eyes," Monty said. "But I don't think gentlemen go around shooting people."

"They do. Just not in public," I said.

"Mostly they get somebody else to do it," Frank said.

As we walked around town, we saw cowboys, sheepherders, farmers, gamblers, businessmen, store clerks, laborers of all kinds, city workers, hotel clerks, and some University of Texas footballers going to practice. We saw women of all sorts. I thought they all looked great wearing all those different kinds of clothes and shoes, with different hairstyles and all sorts of hats: some with feathers, others with poufs of lace, or yards of ribbon, or bouquets of flowers. We passed some Mexicans, one Chinaman, and many more Negroes than you see in the Trans-Pecos, which is almost none.

There were so many telephone, telegraph, and electricity wires that I couldn't count them. It was the first time we saw streets paved with brick, electric streetlights, asphalt paving, and cable cars. On Sixth Street, we came to an impressive building made of brick with limestone accents.

"The Driskill Hotel," Frank said. "I've seen pictures."

We tied our horses to the hitching post and walked into the men's entrance to the hotel. A billiard room, cigar shop, a newsstand, and a barbershop featuring baths flanked a long hallway. All three of us had the same notion. We headed for the baths. After haircuts and shaves, we smelled and looked good. How could the women resist three handsome, virile men? We sauntered to the bar, confident that we'd find beautiful damsels looking for heroic knights to rescue them from their boring lives.

"Whoa," Monty whispered.

The plush leather couches, cowhide barstools, cattle-branded custom carpet, and the grand Texas Longhorn mounted on the wall made me glad we had bathed and shaved. Several groups of men in pairs or triples sipped drinks and talked earnestly with each other. These perfectly coiffured men wearing expensive suits and dress shoes shined stared at us with disdain, then returned to their conversations. Evidently a fresh haircut, shave, and bath weren't good enough for them.

"Don't worry boys," I whispered. "I've seen this type at Yale. Pretentious people are pretenders. They're filled with hot air, but have no steam."

With a bow and a flourish, a young man with a wiggle in his walk and falsetto voice offered us a table near the center of the room. We took one in the back instead. For some reason, this seemed to anger him. After he seated us, he clicked his heals and turned abruptly from us. Perhaps he was unused to rejection.

Frank, as usual, took the chair with his back to the wall. Monty and I sat on either side of him. The three of us positioned ourselves so we could see the entire room, the entrances and the exits. A tall, slim man with an obstinate carriage came to take our orders. His overly large head, a barren globe that had thick eyebrows for a base dominated his features. As he towered above us, his gaze seemed to slide down his nose. I ordered a Jack Daniels on the rocks. This seemed to please him. When Frank asked for lemonade, his rolled eyes mimicked the bald globe of his head. Tufts of hair bristled on the skirts of his bald head at Monty's request for a Dr. Pepper.

After globe-head brought our drinks, substituting a Coca Cola for Monty's order, Frank took a tobacco pouch and a paper tin out of his vest pocket. He pulled a thin piece of paper out of the tin and filled it with tobacco, taking time so as not to spill any. He licked the paper squeezed both ends and rolled the tobacco onto the paper. He admired his work, and then lit the cigarette. He inhaled deeply.

"Where are the women?" Monty asked.

"I'm afraid we've walked into a bar for men only," I said.

"All that cleaning up for nothing," Monty said.

"No," I said. "You only have one time to make a good first impression. Helps to look your best when you see Captain Rogers."

Almost immediately, the conversation turned to guns and shoot-outs. "Most pistol killings happen instantaneous," Frank said. "Like when a couple of drunks get into an argument and start shooting at each other. Each of 'em fires a bunch of shots, and they almost always miss. I mean they miss each other. They are more likely to hit an innocent bystander than their enemy. And they blast the saloon, or wherever they are, all to hell. Breaking up bottles, splintering tables and chairs."

"Wait a minute," I said. "What about when you killed Flores?"

"Case in point," he said. "That wasn't a dime-store-novel gun fight. Flores knew I would arrest him so he went for his gun and I killed him."

"You shot him before he could get his gun out of the holster," I said.

"He was nervous, embarrassed, scared, and he had been drinking. Can't shoot good under those conditions. The winner is almost always the one that's most sober and the one who's got his emotions under control."

"You have to be fast, don't you?" Monty asked. "I mean you shot Flores before he drew his gun."

"Speed generally leads to wild misses, but enough wild shots can kill the best of us. Fortune generally shines on the steady man who kills before the wild shots find their mark," Frank said with a nonchalant shrug.

"Too fast and you miss. Too slow and you die. How did you get it sorted out?" I asked.

"I was always good with a gun," Frank said. "I guess you could say most of my skill came sort of natural. Practice made me confident. Confidence makes me steady. Steadiness makes me fast enough. Fast enough keeps me alive."

"Both then? Both steady and fast," Monty said

"The one who takes his time almost always wins. Flores went for his gun so quick that he didn't get a firm grip on the gun butt. His hand slipped. If he had drawn quicker, speed would have made him unsteady. He would have missed. Steadiness makes you fast."

"People tell me you've killed more than a dozen men," I said

"Most of them Mexicans. They don't count."

"Life sure is short down here on the Rio Grande," I said.

"Pistol whipped more than I shot. Colts are pretty heavy. Make a good club," Frank said.

"I had a Colt Dragoon once. Four pounds. Two ounces. Eight inches," I said.

"The barrel or your private equipment?" Frank asked.

Monty thundered that infectious laugh of his. I chuckled to myself, but didn't say anything. The bar began to fill up with impressive looking patrons. The three of us decided that we liked what we saw in Austin, but didn't want to see it all the time. We didn't like the noise, the crowds, and the smells. All three of us hated the automobile. We had seen and heard enough. It was time to move on.

Frank threw a couple of silver dollars on the table, and we walked out of the Driskill. We rode west on Sixth Street, and in half a block, we intersected with Congress Avenue. With our backs to the Colorado River, we looked up the slope of Congress Avenue and saw an enormous red granite building resting on top of a gentle rise.

"See that red granite building on top of that hill," I said.

"Looks like pictures I've seen of the U.S. Capital," Monty said with admiration.

"Only bigger. Seventh largest building in the world." I said. "The Texas Capitol."

We rode away as Monty headed for the Capital—and a meeting with Captain Rogers. As he was leaving, Frank called after him, "Monty, when you get your Texas Ranger badge, come see me. I need someone who can shoot a pistol and not have to use a short barrel shotgun to hit anything."

"Samuel Colt made all men equal. This shotgun changes the equation," I retorted. I turned toward Monty. "I expect you will be a law and order man just like Charlie Goodnight," I said with a smile.

Monty responded with a wink and a tip of the hat.

Chapter 5

FRANK AND I SAT in Captain John H. Rodgers' sumptuous office on the second floor of the Texas Capitol. An enormous map of Texas dominated the west wall. From his desk, Captain Rodgers could see the South Congress Avenue Bridge that crossed the Colorado River. Monty had been assigned to Company B in Northeast Texas under the tutelage of Buckner Fanning. If he passed scrutiny, he would be officially sworn in as a Texas Ranger.

Captain Rodgers thanked Frank for recommending Monty. "He talks a lot, but he is a law and order man. No one can bribe him. He'll excuse no favorites," he said.

Captain Rogers was a polite, soft-spoken man. Short, stocky with graying hair and wearing glasses, he reminded me of a banker rather than a Texas Ranger. His reputation belied his appearance. An extraordinarily brave and deeply religious man who carried a Bible in his saddlebag, Rodgers believed alcohol contributed to most crimes. After joining the Rangers as an 18-year-old, he had been in numerous gun battles. Twice, he received severe wounds. A right shoulder wound left his arm shortened so he carried a specially constructed Winchester into battle. Frank, who idolized Captain Rogers, told me that he tried to be like him.

"If you love danger, Navasota is the place to find it," Captain Rogers said. "The violence in Navasota may be the most severe of any Texas town, including the Trans Pecos."

Goody, I thought.

"Governor Campbell passed a letter to me from Gladys Shine, daughter of Peter Welsh Shine of Navasota. Mr. Shine contributed thousands to Governor Campbell's campaign." Captain Rogers pulled the letter from his desk, cleared his throat, and read it aloud. Then he put down the letter, took off his glasses, and began wiping them with a tissue. "I checked with Ranger Sergeant John Dibrell who I sent to Navasota last year. His report wasn't as melodramatic as Miss Shine's, but he essentially confirmed her letter. He told me that over 100 people had been murdered in Grimes County in the past two years."

"What's the population of Navasota?" Frank asked.

"3,200 people," Rogers replied.

I whistled. "That's a murder for every 32 people," I said. "That figure is hard to believe."

Captain Rogers and Frank nodded in agreement. We sat there contemplating those figures.

"I know Dibrell. Worked with him in Terlingua, near Big Bend. He's not the type to exaggerate," Frank said. "But still, that number of murders seems awfully high."

"Sodom and Gomorrah numbers," I said.

"Navasota's three railroads provide the shipping hub for Grimes County and some of the surrounding counties. Lots of people coming and going ... and it's difficult to know how many Negroes work on those huge plantations," Captain Rogers said. "Most likely, the violence will escalate. City Marshal Loftin resigned last month when he got his finger shot off trying to stop a gunfight," Rogers said.

"Who's in charge now?" Frank asked.

"Robert Spurger runs the town. Both Dibrell and Loftin used the same noun to describe him. They both called him a 'fiend.'"

"Interesting," I said. "Miss Shine used fiendish in her letter." No one commented.

"Spurger is the mayor of Navasota and the largest landowner. He has all the power and money any sane man would want, but he keeps fomenting trouble..." Rogers paused, then added, almost to himself, "why?"

All of us sat there for a while saying nothing. Then Frank spoke, "He needs Negroes to work in the cotton fields. Cultivating the land and picking cotton is back-breaking work. No one would pick cotton unless they absolutely had to. Spurger suppresses Negros so they have no choice but to work for him and the other plantation owners."

"Exactly," Rogers said. "Spurger knows how to manipulate politics to whip up dissension and keep the Negroes from exercising their freedom. He is a master of confusion and deception."

"Complicated political issues make distinguishing the good guys from the bad especially difficult," Frank said.

"Can't tell the white hats from the black hats," I said.

"To understand Navasota and Grimes County politics, let's review some history," Rogers said.

He took a sip of water from his glass and from a pitcher of water on his desk filled two glasses for Frank and me. I would have preferred Jack Daniel's but didn't say anything. A couple of shots of whiskey make politics more digestible. After three shots, you may not understand the issues, but you don't care. While I contemplated the benefits of Jack Daniel's, Rogers began again.

"After the Civil War Republicans made certain that the blacks had the right to vote. As a spin-off, the Negroes, tenant farmers, sharecroppers, and the underprivileged formed the People's Party. Gradually, the Democrats gained enough influence to enact Jim Crow laws that called for a poll tax. The poll tax required citizens to pay a relatively small sum of money to be eligible to vote. The blacks and the poor whites didn't have the money for the poll tax. Landowners, wealthy merchants, and the more affluent whites gained power. In Navasota, Spurger organized the White Man's Union to support the tax. From that came the local Ku Klux Klan."

Rogers paused to see if we understood. Both of us nodded for him to go on.

"Before the White Man's League gained power, The People's Party elected Garrett Scott to be City Marshal of Navasota," Rogers said. He paused, and gazed out the window. "He served as Navasota Marshal for over twenty years."

"Why Scott? What made him popular with the Negros?" I asked.

"The Negroes liked Scott because he and his relatives were … I guess you would say … enlightened plantation owners," Rogers said with a shrug. "They took care of their slaves. Treated them right. When the blacks were freed, Scott allowed them to sharecrop some of his land. Spurger attempted to keep Navasota merchants from selling products to those who refused to join the Democratic Party," Rogers said. "With complete control over the impoverished whites and the Negroes, he could replace Scott with a puppet marshal."

"A 'fiend' does seem the best way to describe Spurger," I said.

Most of the Navasota merchants didn't agree with Spurger's attempt because it cut into their profits. A few went along with Spurger's manipulations," Rogers said taking a sip of water. "The hardware store owner and the Vice President of the White Man's Union, Bill McDonald, refused to sell some nails to a tenant farmer surnamed Windom. The farmer threw a fit. When Windom realized his screaming and hollering didn't get him the nails he wanted, he pulled out a pocket gun and shot McDonald in the face."

"For the lack of a nail, the battle was lost," I said.

"It didn't take long for Spurger to take advantage of the situation," Rogers said. "Spurger has two thugs that do most of his dirty work—Pack Hardy and the gunslinger, Whip Wilson. He had them roust an all-white mob."

"I've heard of Wilson," Frank said. "Claims to be the fastest gun east of the Trans Pecos."

"Hardy shot two black leaders in the back. Wilson gunned down the Marshal's brother, Emmett Lee Scott and killed Deputy John Bradley with two dead-center chest shots. Some unknown assailant shot Scott in front of the jail. His niece threw herself over him. As bullets rained down from nearby buildings, she somehow drug him into the jailhouse where some men and women had taken cover. Constant gunfire pinned all of them in the jailhouse for several days. Someone sent a telegram to the governor. The state militia rescued them. Scott died of his wounds a few months later. Navasota has been lawless since," Rogers sat back breathless.

"I think I'll need more shotgun shells before we leave for Navasota," I said.

Chapter 6

A CLICK OF THE TONGUE and a light kick in the sides encouraged our horses to canter toward Navasota. All of us—horses and men—were glad to get away from that crowded and noisy city. The freshness of the country air and the beauty of a spring day glowing with multicolored flowers, budding trees, and thigh-high green grass stretching as far as we could see made us feel complacent and content and better satisfied with life.

We walked our horses along a road that climbed up a slow gradual slope, dipping to cross gulleys and creeks then gradually climbing again. At the top of the hill, we paused and looked around. In every direction, we saw a limitless expanse of green prairie dotted with bluebonnets, Indian Paint Brush, and other wild flowers. As we started down a winding slope and onto the prairie, a soft breeze kept us cool.

— • —

With night coming on, we dismounted, unsaddled, and groomed our horses with currycombs that we carried in our saddlebags. We watered our horses in a small spring-fed creek and let them run free in a grassy area, certain that they were trained to return to us when called.

I gathered some flat stones and circled them around a small crater that

I had scratched out of the topsoil. After that I constructed a spit by hanging a greenstick over the fire pit, supported by two forked limbs I had cut, shaped, and driven into the ground. I gathered some deadfall and with matches and the tinder from my saddlebag soon had a crackling and popping fire going.

I got the whiskey flask out of my saddlebag, took a big swig, and passed the flask to Frank. He put the flask to his lips, but I don't think he drank any. If he did, it was the littlest of sips. He returned the flask to me.

"Sounds like Navasota treats Negroes like the border towns treat Mexicans," I said.

"Mexicans are different. They're murdering thieves, smugglers, and rustlers. They deserve to be shot," Frank growled.

I didn't mention anything about bias or a double standard. My shotgun wasn't handy, and I didn't want to be kicked all the way to the creek. Mama didn't raise no dumb boy as the saying goes, I thought. Instead, I said, "You seem to be partial to blacks."

"One of 'em saved my life. I'm inclined to 'em," Frank said. He had that familiar faraway look when talking of the past. "I was 16; my brother, Harrison, 12. We were sharecropping for this mean old codger, Dan McSween, a cross-eyed scrawny old man with hair sticking out every which way like straw in a hay barn. Stick him to a pole and he would have made a great scarecrow."

I chuckled at the imagery.

"McSween was as creepy as a tarantula and as vicious as a cornered bobcat," Frank said. "Old man McSween knew I was good with a gun. He had seen me shoot birds out of the sky with my Winchester. He asked me to kill a rancher who he suspected of grazing cattle on his land. I thought he was joking at first, but I realized he was serious when he offered $200 for the job. I told him I wasn't a killer for hire."

Frank looked at me. His jutted chin and penetrating eyes expressed a resolved tenacity.

"I went to the rancher's house and warned him about McSween. I figured it was all over. Harrison and I continued to work McSween's land. About a week after McSween's request, we were planting seeds in his field. Harrison saw that skunk sneaking up on me and screamed, 'Look out he's aiming at you.'"

Frank's voice rose to a crescendo.

"I jumped to one side. The first shot missed. Then I started running. McSween fired the second barrel, and buckshot slammed into my back and the left side of my head. I fell bleeding but managed to pull my pocket pistol and fire shots wildly in his direction. One must have hit him because he fell. Then he got up and hobbled into his house."

I threw some logs on the dying fire and stirred-up the embers. The logs caught. The licking flames brought a little warmth to us. I took a couple of big gulps out of the whiskey flask. Once again, Frank refused the whiskey. The tables were turned. Frank drinks like a preacher while I, an ex-preacher, drink like gunslinger. Frank looked up at the stars and began again.

"Harrison ran toward me and managed to pull me up. I leaned on him, and with him dragging me, we made it over a hill and hid in a ravine. After a while, here comes McSween riding a horse, carrying a buffalo gun looking for us, but we were tucked under some thick yaupon and muscadine vines, and he didn't see us. We waited until we thought it was safe. I crawled with Harrison tugging me until we came upon a small rutted road. Just as we got there, a Negro man came around a bend in the road, driving a wagon. By this time, I was bleeding badly. Somehow Harrison and the colored man got me in the wagon, and he drove me to the doctor."

I leaned forward listening intently, watching the blue and yellow and red flames flicker in the fire.

"By the time we got to the doctor, I had lost so much blood that I was in and out of consciousness. Somehow the doc dug out some of the buckshot and got the bleeding stopped. I remembered him telling my Pa and Ma that because of all the blood loss, I had no chance to make it. I was so weak, I couldn't say anything. I lay there with the room spinning round and round. I passed out or went to sleep or was delirious or something and I saw this angel—had wings almost as wide as the room with shimmering and shining bright light all around. The angel told me ... not really in words ... I felt it more than I heard it, but the idea, or thought, or whatever you call it was clear as spring water. The angel said ... er, communicated ... that the love of Jesus and Holy Spirit Power would heal me. Then I passed out completely, and I didn't remember anything for two or three weeks. It took me almost six months to get all my strength back."

The fire was dying down turning the coals into ashes. Just like our lives. The fierce flames of youth slowly flicker out.

"You see why I favor the blacks," Frank said. "If it weren't for that colored man, all my blood would have seeped away in that dusty road. That Negro saved my life. Because of that man, I am living today."

We both sat there for a while until I said, "I guess you had two angels— a wagon driving black one and a wide-winged white one."

"Yes," Frank said. "Destiny saved me. That's why I fear no one and no thing. Our time will come when fate decides—it will come on our appointed day. There's nothing we can do to change it. Those two angels taught me that. I know this for sure," Frank said. "God doesn't make anybody smarter than him. All the theology books in the world aren't going to explain God and why things happen the way they do because God knows and we don't. Yes, God knows and we don't, so I don't try to figure out things that muddy my mind. You got to take some things on faith. Faith will save you."

"You sound like a Pentecostal rattlesnake-charming preacher," I said.

Frank didn't laugh; instead I saw a flash of anger in his eyes. He was hurt. He was talking seriously, and I was making light of it. I tried to recover his trust quickly, "I'm sorry. I shouldn't have said that. It just came rolling off my tongue. Sometimes my tongue starts up before my brain has time to stop it."

Frank didn't say anything at first. He just looked at me with those cold, snake-like eyes. I saw that stare just before he started kicking the hell out of someone who wronged him or hurt someone else. In less than a beat, that killer stare was replaced by warm, understanding eyes. That rattlesnake stare went away so quickly that most people wouldn't have seen it. But I'd seen it. It's a stare you don't forget, and one that you can't afford to miss. You got to jump out of a rattlesnake's path before it strikes. Same with Frank: Jump out of the way when you see that stare.

I doused the fire and untied my bedroll from the saddle cantle. I turned the saddle on its side with the stirrups away from me and used the saddle seat for a headrest. I closed my eyes, thinking about Frank and the complexity of being human. Most of us act differently during stressful times, but those reactions are subtle shades of gray. Frank had two distinct temperaments, not exactly Jekyll and Hyde differences, but extremes nonetheless. The warm, compassionate, intelligent side quickly transforms into the raging, beastly side when he recognizes injustice. I cherished his friendship. I never wanted to be his enemy.

I opened my eyes. Frank stood gazing heavenward. The full moon gave his face a translucent glow.

"We will be up against the plantation owners, the bankers, and the community leaders who want to keep their power. Spurger and his city council may accept us at first because Governor Campbell sent us, but they will do everything they can to stop us. Big trouble is coming, and we're bringing it," Frank said softly, almost to himself.

Chapter 7

WE RODE INTO NAVASOTA. Frank sat deep in the saddle, bearing part of his weight on the stirrups, swaying left and right in rhythm with his horse, Bugler. He wore a high-crowned Stetson with a wide brim. A wide leather belt with loops for 50 cartridges held a .45 Colt sheathed in a double loop Ranger holster. He had his backup weapon, a .44 Smith and Wesson, tucked under his belt. A Savage Model 1899 rested in a rifle sheath secured to his saddle. My straw Stetson angled down to protect my eyes from the sun. A linen shirt and tan brushed cotton pants kept me as cool as possible in the Texas heat. A saddle holster held my takedown 12-gauge.

We dismounted, secured Bugler and Warrior to a hitching post outside the city hall, and walked upstairs to an expansive conference room where three men waited for our arrival. Frank and I entered the room, paused just inside the door, and looked around.

The men sat at a long mahogany desk in side-armed leather chairs. Three other empty chairs surrounded the desk. A hat tree was in the corner of the room adjacent to the door. Two wooden filing cabinets at the distant corner sat next to a small bookcase containing what appeared to be bound city records and official documents. A chart of the town and a large map of the county adorned the back wall. A wide front window looked out on Main Street over the roofs of other houses beyond and onto the grassland prairie stretching to the river. The eastward looking window gave a view of the wide boulevard as it reached out to a rutted road disappearing into a pine forest.

Frank nodded at the men and took off his hat. "Name's Frank Hamer," he said.

"We know who you are. Governor Campbell sent you here and told us to give you free reign," the man sitting at the far end of the mahogany desk said. He was dressed in a dark business suit. He had dark brown irises, so dark that they obscured his pupils. His thin, compressed lips gave him a flinty, churlish look.

"I'm Robert Spurger, the Mayor of this town," he said indignantly. "I'm also President of the Brazos Bank, and a landowner. Clearing out the riffraff that hazards our town's economy is both a community and a personal concern for me."

Spurger's supercilious smile made me want to puke. Many times, I have been fooled by first impressions, but my stomach told me this wasn't one of those times. He was more than smarmy; he was sinister.

"Governor Campbell and Captain Rogers may have assigned you to our little town, but we are going to evaluate you on our own terms," he said with a sardonic smile. "If we don't like what we hear, we will ask the governor to send someone else."

Spurger paused for a few beats. He wanted us to know he controlled the room.

With a wave of his hand toward the man on his right he said, "The aldermen sitting here with me can introduce themselves."

"Pike Ravil," a hunch-shouldered man said without inflection. The lines running perpendicular from his mouth and his round jowled face gave him a mirthless look. "I own the cottonseed oil mill south of town. It's the first one in Texas."

"Howdy I'm Oscar Bauer. I own the livery in town." He was a short man wearing a Stetson with a ridge-top crown to make him look taller. His wrinkled and grim, narrow-face reminded me of a dried fig. He dressed nothing like the liverymen I knew. He wore a suede jacket over a white dress shirt. His tie was Windsor knotted. Bitterness crossed Bauer's face. "We were hoping to get Dibrell back. Lots of experience."

"Dibrell was the kind of man we thought we could work with: nice, easy going. He seemed to understand our plans. Just after he got settled, Captain Rogers called him back to Alpine. Chico Cano and his banditos had been stealing horses in Texas and selling them in Mexico. We requested his return. Dibrell said he didn't want to be penned in one place. Didn't like the humidity and mosquitoes in East Texas. Liked being a Texas Ranger better. Open spaces," Ravil said.

A young Mexican woman with a yellow rose penned in her straight, raven hair entered the room carrying a tray containing a coffee urn and three cups. She put the tray on the table, turned, and left the room. Her tight dress entranced me. She walked with a bewitching shimmer. She glanced over her shoulder and looked at me, then closed the door and disappeared. Spurger filled the three cups with steaming coffee.

No one offered Frank a chair. He stood. His left hand rested on his hip with his leg slightly bent at the knee. His gun hand dangled below his holster barely touching his firmly anchored leg. I remained near the door.

"Awful young looking," Bauer said in a loud voice as if we weren't there.

"Big boy though. What? Six-three? Muscled. Looks like he could throw a mule," Ravil said without acknowledging us.

"But can he shoot?" Bauer asked.

Anger flushed Frank's face but disappeared as quickly as it appeared. His right hand moved ever so slightly, toward his Colt. The aldermen's patronizing comments disgusted me.

"Got a letter here from Captain Rogers. Says he can," Spurger said.

"What do you say, boy? Can you shoot?" asked Bauer.

All three men looked at Frank.

"No one has outshot me yet," Frank said with a lopsided grin, ignoring the 'boy' reference. Unasked, he eased into the chair at the opposite end from Spurger.

"We've had over fifty murders in the last year. What can you do about that?" Ravil asked.

"There's a list of city rules that I will post all over town. If the townspeople and visitors follow the rules, everything will be muy bueno," Frank said with a nonchalant look.

Spurger stirred in his seat. "And if they don't?" he asked.

Frank looked perfectly relaxed as he sat comfortably in the chair, hands in his lap, an ironic gaze in his eyes. "Then I'll arrest them."

"What if they resist?" Bauer asked with a touch of sarcasm in his voice.

"Then I'll kick them all the way to the jail."

The men laughed. All three had astonished looks on their faces. "You going to punt them like in that college football game they play," Bauer said still laughing.

"Or kick the can," Ravil said with a grin.

I stepped forward. I'd had enough of these condescending comments and mocking questions. "He's a Savate Foot fighter," I said, my disgust aimed at the three men.

This brought more derisive laughter and dismissive looks.

"*Savate*—French for boot. He kicks the hell out of those who get in his way," I said. "Has twists, moves, jumps, and trips that no one expects. Takes 'em by surprise. A quick kick in the groin usually does it."

Spurger glanced at the other aldermen and looked out the window as two gnarled men walked out of the Copperhead Saloon. Both of them were carrying. He returned his gaze to Frank and raised his eyebrows. "What if they draw on you first?"

"Probably kill me."

"He's been fast enough so far," I said.

"There's always someone out there who is faster. The first time you meet them is the last time," Frank said.

"You don't seem very confident," Bauer said.

"Confidence. That's a tricky word. Does confidence mean certainty—against what? Self-assurance—against whom? Conviction—where? Belief—when? Poise—Why? Does it indicate optimism or recklessness?" Frank asked with irritation in his voice.

Clearly, he had had enough of their patronizing.

"I prefer fearless," Frank continued. "I know there are many out there who can kill me in a gunfight ... or they can ambush me, knife me, or hang me. But I don't go around worrying about it. When someone threatens me, my family, my friends, my town, I destroy the vermin with no remorse. I don't back down. I crusade against evil in whatever form it takes. I'll never betray that mission. The good Lord knows when it's my time to go. When he's ready, I'm ready. So I fight with no fear in my heart. Fearless is a better word."

Frank leaned forward putting his hands on the table. His sparkling eyes turned a steely blue as he stared at each man and held their eyes until they turned away. He had seized control of the room. A deadly silence surrounded us. For the first time, I became aware of sounds from the street below—carriages passing, a dog barking, the creak of a wagon, the clap of hooves.

After a moment, Frank said, "If I can't boot them, or pummel them, or outdraw them, my partner will shoot them. Jude McAbee. He's standing by the door."

"Heard of him," Spurger said. "Carries a riot gun."

"Cut down," Frank said.

"Wait a minute," Bauer said. "You're proposing to end the murders in Navasota by killing people?"

"Maybe yes. Maybe no. The law is the solution. Sometimes killing is the only way to get people obeying the law," Frank said. He shrugged his shoulders. His face had softened into a relaxed, friendly look.

The three men sat silently for a moment, deep in thought. Perhaps they had never encountered a man quite like him.

"We got two groups here in Navasota. The White Man's Union and the Populist—the People's Party they call themselves—mostly Negros with a few sharecroppers, sheep herders, and day workers," Ravil said.

"You side with one, the other will go after you. There'll be five ... ten men gunning for you as soon as you put on the Marshal's badge," Bauer said.

"Maybe more," Frank said.

"You goin' to kill'em all!" Ravil exclaimed.

"That will be up to them," Frank said.

Spurger glanced both at Ravil and Bauer. They gave despondent shrugs. "Well, that settles it then. Governor Campbell sent you, and you've answered our questions. Now we'll see what you can do," Spurger said with an incredibly contemptuous grin of utter hostile malevolence.

Frank looked into Spurger's eyes with burning intensity. He leaned even further forward and spread his arms the width of the table. "Yes, if your terms meet my terms, I will be Marshal of Navasota, and Jude will be my deputy. You will find that threats have no power over us. Our strength comes from God."

No one said anything. After what seemed like a minute or two, but was probably only a few seconds, Ravil pulled out some legal looking material from a leather attaché. Bauer asked, "What are your expectations?"

I never cared for back and forth negotiations. I left the paper shuffling with Frank. I abhor legalese. The terms whereof, herewith, and thereof are used by attorneys to confuse and discombobulate. I bowed out and went looking for the senorita with the beguiling allure.

Chapter 8

I FOUND THE ENTRANCING woman in the kitchen. She had an irresistible aura—a glow of innocence mixed with undaunted pride. Her warmth drew me toward her. As I approached, she looked up at the ceiling toward the conference room we came from. I realized that she had a death-like fear of Spurger.

I extended my hand toward her. She took it tenderly. "Don't be afraid of Spurger. I will protect you," I said. She was about to speak. I put my hand over her mouth. "Shush," I whispered.

I bent toward her. She stood on her tiptoes to receive my kiss. Just as our lips met, the cook walked into the room. She jumped, startled. Our passion collapsed.

The cook looked away. He began pulling pots off the shelf. I started to ask the beguiling woman when we could meet again. I looked toward the cook. I decided not to ask.

I gave her a longing, loving glace. She returned my gaze. The cook began chopping vegetables. He seemed oblivious to what had happened. I left.

When I returned from my tryst, I found Frank at the jailhouse learning back in a swivel chair. He had his extended legs crossed at the ankles with his booted feet on the desk. He took his feet off the table and put the book down.

I looked around. The cedar walls had no decoration. No wanted posters. No calendar. A Franklin stove sat in the right corner opposite a cheap beige couch. In the center of the room, two straight back chairs sat in front of an overly large oil-stained pine desk, allowing plenty of room for a typewriter, telephone, papers, and Frank's large feet. A four-drawer filling cabinet, a small safe, and gun rack sat against the back wall. There were four jail cells on the right side of the hall that led to the back door with a wooden water bucket, dipper, and a couple of cups sitting on a small table opposite the cells.

"The cells are empty," I said.

"We'll fill them."

"I have three occupants in mind," I said. "Spurger, Ravil, and Bauer."

"All we lack is evidence." Frank shrugged.

"Spurger is ... creepy," I said. "When I pursued the killer Robert Lowry, he escaped into the Big Thicket east of Livingston. My Indian guide and I were in a canoe on the Neches. The muddy, narrow river that blended into swampy water had Spanish moss hanging from the trees touching our face. We must have come across a cottonmouth nest because a huge moccasin attacked our canoe and tried to slither into the boat. The guide beat the cottonmouth off with his paddle. Spurger reminds me of that moccasin."

"I got the same menacing feeling, but I don't believe Spurger attacks," Frank said. "He is more like a hyena. He waits for others to kill and then devours the carcass. Spurger uses others to do his deviltry." Frank shrugged in a nonchalant way. "Spurger's principle weapon is fear. God gives us power over fear." He put his feet back on the desk. Before he picked up the book to return to reading, I noticed the title, *Roughing It*.

"So you like Mark Twain?" I asked with no preamble.

Frank looked up. His eyes twinkled. "I've read *Huckleberry Finn* and *Tom Sawyer*. This is my favorite. Read it three times."

"I'm impressed," I said pulling up a chair.

"What? You didn't think Texas Rangers could read?" he asked with a crooked smile.

"I just didn't think you would read that much. You being a Ranger and all."

"The only education I got was on the hurricane end of a Mexican pony," he said. "But every Texas family has one book. The Bible taught me to read. Thought I was going to be a preacher."

"What turned you?" I asked

"Wilbarger's book *Indian Depredations in Texas* made me want to be an Indian," he said with that crooked smile still on his face.

"Just about every Texan has read that book. Maybe more read it than the Bible," I said. "I've discovered that people find the Bible more useful for killing spiders or keeping a door from swinging open than they do for learning about the good Lord and his mysterious ways."

"You may be right," he said with a chuckle. "And I guess you could say that Wilbarger's book became a Bible for me."

"*Indian Depredations in Texas* is about the Comanche torturing, scalping, raping and murdering Texas settlers ... and it made you want to become an Indian? That's strange," I said feeling more comfortable with this young Ranger by the day. I walked over to the water bucket and while talking, filled two cups with water. I put one cup on Frank's desk. I sat down and took a sip out of my cup.

"The Comanche raids followed a pattern that terrified the settlers. The men that weren't killed were castrated in front of the women, scalped, and then tortured in ghastly, grisly, gruesome ways that challenge the imagination. All the babies were killed. The women were repeatedly raped, scalped, and shot with arrows. Sometimes young kids were captured and used as slaves."

"There was a method to their madness," Frank said. "The Comanche thought harrowing tales of their cruelty would drive the settlers away. Only the Texas Rangers and the forbearance, doggedness and pertinacity of the pioneers helped them stand firm against the Comanche who were determined to keep their land."

"The faint-hearted fled," I said. "The bold and the brave remained."

"Texas grit," Frank said.

"I still don't understand why you would want to be a Comanche," I said shifting in my chair. It made an awful screech.

Frank took several big swigs of his water. I looked out the window. The town buzzed with activity. "I saw the Comanche as sort of a cavalier swooping down unexpectedly from the distant plains protecting their land from intruders and then retreating before any effective pursuit could be made. I guess the Comanche appealed to the crusading part of me ... or perhaps the aggressive, combative, militant side of me."

"I have a killer side and a preacher side," I said. "I suppose you have a preacher side too. Most of us do. Just about all of us have a good side and a bad side, fighting it out for our attention. Some people though are pure evil ... I've never thought of this before, but maybe we use our evil side to fight evil."

"You got a ten-gallon way of thinking: too big for my head," Frank said standing up and walking to the window. "All I know is when I read Wilbarger's book, I decided I wanted to be as much like an Indian as possible. When I was a boy, I lived in the woods whenever I could. I had my Winchester, fishing gear, and bowie knife. I lived off the land. Made shelters. Slept on the ground. Learned all about animals and birds. Learned to call deer, fox, quail, turkey, and duck. A fox makes a wap-wap-wap sound and yips and squeals; sometimes it barks like a dog but with a lower pitch. A deer makes a soft consistent grunt when wanting a mate or a friend. The mockingbird makes a hell of a racket whenever a predator is around. If I heard those sharp rasps and scolds, I began looking for cougars, wolves, and the like. Nature taught—and book taught. I read a bunch of books when I was out there in the woods, listening, soaking up the wildness."

"What kind of books?"

"Adventure books mostly: *Robertson Caruso, Treasure Island. The Call of the Wild.* And I studied up on the Bible. Read a little of Shakespeare's *Sonnets.* That was a little too tough for me."

"Shakespeare is rough reading. Took some studying to figure out the language, but now I favor it. Shakespeare and the Bible teach the rhythm of words."

"If you talk like that in the saloons, you'll be shot, sure," Frank said.

Chapter 9

"I'M LUKE CLEMONS, publisher of the *Navasota Examiner-Review*," a tall, slim man said when he entered the office. He wore black garters over the sleeves of a blue pinstripe shirt with an open collar. He had ink stains on his fingers and under his nails. A full head of black hair topped his high forehead. Large blue-green eyes gave him an inquisitive look. He looked to be somewhere around 40 years old.

"I'd like to put an article in the paper about y'all coming to Navasota," he said. After he had filled a couple of sheets of paper in his notebook with our answers to his innocuous questions, he thanked us and left.

In the early afternoon, Frank pinned his Marshal badge on his leather vest, and I put on my Deputy badge. We took a tour of the town both to survey the surroundings, show a lawful presence, and to post our Navasota City Rules. The sky was perfectly blue and cloudless. A cool breeze seemed to reduce the sun's burning heat.

Frank had his big Colt on his side holster and his Smith & Wesson tucked in his cartridge-filled belt. Even though I couldn't shoot straight, I also wore a holstered Colt strapped to my side, Johnny Ringo style. I thought I looked pretty dangerous. We wanted to show authority and our seriousness of upholding the law. At the same time, we wanted to be cordial and ask casual questions.

"The more you ask in a friendly way, the faster people will reveal themselves," Frank said as he tipped his hat to a clerk loading a wagon with groceries. "Being friendly with everyone has brought me success with informants. Often people with menial jobs, the poor, drunks, and loafers that hang around don't do much of anything, but they do listen. People I've favored or who want a favor have been great sources of information: outlaws who've turned, jailbirds and thugs to whom I've shown leniency."

At every store and with every person we met, Frank came across as a friendly brother or son. He walked with a lazy, rolling gait. He was gracious and polite. His radiant, full-faced smile, twinkling eyes, infectious laugh, and his listening skills made instantaneous friends.

A few loafers roosted on benches scattered around the town. They generally had on wide-brimmed straw hats, denim overalls with khaki shirts, and brown lace-up boots. They spoke lazy and draggy of nothing important; although, an impressive assortment of cusswords would make it seem otherwise. They were a minority group. We met a lot more doers and achievers—go-getters on the go and glad handers with beatific smiles.

Buggies, wagons, coaches, and dozens of horses tied to hitching posts lined the street. The afternoon crowd bustled along the walkways. Most all the women wore sunbonnets; some of the younger ladies wore bustle skirts; the older women had on calico dresses with children in tow. Booted cowboys, spurs jingling, paraded in and out of the saloons joined by a considerable number of farmers in their coveralls. An undertaker ... I guessed ... dressed in black with a tailcoat entered the Throop Saloon. A couple of railroad men stood on the corner talking. We saw businessmen, bankers perhaps and maybe an attorney or two in dark Edwardian suits. There were bunches of blacks all trying to avoid contact with the whites.

"There're more blacks here than Mexicans up and down the Rio Grande," I said.

"You have a great talent for exaggerating," Frank said. "But, yes, there are about as many blacks as whites in Navasota. Look at the way they bow and scrape to the white people. Get off the boardwalk when they see a white man coming. Avoid eye contact with a white woman. They are whipped down. Disgusting. We'll fix that. It may take time, but we'll fix it."

"Everybody deserves respect and should be allowed to make it in their own way," I said. "Whites ... Blacks ... Mexicans."

Frank frowned when I said "Mexicans," but I ignored it.

Washington Street provided a wide thoroughfare. A wooden walkway paralleled both sides of the street. As we stopped at each building to post our City Rules, we met and greeted the citizens. There were perhaps twenty or so buildings on both sides of the street, mostly framed, some stone, a few bricked. Almost all the framed buildings were painted white with colorful awnings hanging over them.

At least a dozen saloons were scattered throughout downtown, already doing a brisk business in the early afternoon. A large post office with cement steps leading to the entrance dominated the adjacent corner of Main Street in the middle of town.

The Brazos Bank and Loan had an iron filigree fence fronting a porch. The Lone Star Bank with exterior walls of Texas granite soared two stories high west of the square and across the railroad tracks. On the north side of Main Street and across from the Lone Star Bank sat Oscar Bauer's Livery Feed and Seed Store.

On Railroad Street east of the tracks the train depot bustled with activity. Two towers contained telephone and telegraph areas, and signal operations. The towers rose two stories topped by peaked roofs. South of the towers, loading docks separated storage buildings from the railroad tracks.

Frank and I examined a wood-framed armory abutting the nearest storage building. Inside, rifles, shotguns, and pistols of all kinds and shapes shared space with boxes full of ammunition, gunpowder, and dynamite.

"A match and a little gasoline would blow this building all the way to Houston," Frank said.

There was a doctor's office with "Leonard O. Coleman, MD" painted on the window. Rucker's Drug Store nestled between Smith's Hotel and a dental office. Ahrenbeck and Terrell Hardware, Cashmore's General Merchandize, Long's grocery store, and Farquhar Meat Market were on the other side of the street.

"People sure are proud of their names here," I said.

We entered Cashmore's General Merchandise. Mr. Cashmore introduced himself and proudly showed us around his store crammed with goods of all kinds. Whiskey was prominently displayed. Calico, crepe, candles, Bauer oil, needles and thread, ropes and harnesses, tobacco, cooking pots, cheese and pickled fish, bolts, and other hardware items crammed every inch of available space. Barrels brimmed with sugar, vinegar, flour, and molasses. Canisters contained condiments and spices, and big glass jars of striped candy sticks.

As we were leaving, Mr. Cashmore offered both of us cigar shaped objects wrapped in wax paper. "Have a Tootsie Roll," he said. "It's quickly becoming a best seller. It's sort of like a combination of taffy and caramel. Can chew it for a long time without making a mess. Doesn't melt in the sun—cowboys love it. They put it in their saddlebags and chew on it when they need a boost of energy."

We thanked him for the candy and were leaving the store when Mr. Cashmore stopped us again.

"Hope you boys have come here for the right reason. We need to get rid of some of the niggers and white trash around here. They have no money to spend, and they crowd out the people who want to buy something."

When the door closed behind us, we looked at each other, puzzled.

"That's a different slant on things," I said as I bit into the Tootsie Roll—chewy and sweet—but I didn't like the way the candy stuck to my teeth.

We crossed the street to check out a two-story brick building, the Rucker Drug Store. All sorts of medicines were displayed in the store. On the shelves, we saw Mandrake Pills, Liver and Stomach Corrector; Spanish

Catarrh Cure, Taylor's Cherokee Remedy and several other products containing laudanum with 10% opium; Carter's Little Liver Pills, Pinkham's Vegetable Compound, and Lilly's Aphrodisiac Pills; Hepatica manufactured by Bristol-Myers, Listerine Antiseptic, and Johnson and Johnson bandages. Toothpaste in a tube rested behind a shelf. We noticed Ogden's Guinea Gold Cigarettes, and bottled Coca-Cola, too. When I saw the Dr Pepper bottles, I smiled remembering our chatterbox friend, Monty, the law and order idealist—I missed him already.

Mr. Rucker came over and introduced himself. "Heard you boys were in town. Need to put some of the niggers in place so the good white folks will feel safe. They'll stop going to Courtney, and spend their money here."

Frank and I glanced at each other. Maybe the merchants had the wrong idea about our being here.

"The streets seem booming to me. Looks like business is good, very good," I said.

"Business can never be good enough," Mr. Rucker said. "We're counting on you to do what's right so we will keep our businesses going."

"Thank you, sir," Frank said, tipping his hat, a paragon of unassuming modesty. "We'll need your help. If you hear or suspect anything, come tell Jude or me. The more information we can get, the better we can control this town," Frank said with a smile on his face, not revealing our true purpose for being in Navasota.

"I sure hope you can clean up this town. Nobody else has been able to," Mr. Rucker replied.

"Jude and his takedown have a way making people real polite," Frank said.

Chapter 10

A WOMAN IN HER 50S, Kandy Canola, owner of Kandy's Kitchen, who looked like she enjoyed her products, introduced herself with almost the same wishes that Mr. Rucker expressed. Frank assured her that we would do our very best to bring peace to the streets of Navasota.

"Let me show you our latest addition," she said. "Ta-dah! A brine ice cream making machine. The machine can make 75 gallons of ice cream an hour. A two-horse power gasoline engine runs the ice cream maker, and it powers three large fans that keep the ice cream and the store cool. The ice cream comes in every flavor as long as it is vanilla."

Kandy grinned as she served us both two large scoops of ice cream in a small cup. We ate voraciously with many oohs and ahs.

"I sell lots of ice cream to the crowds watching the hangings," Kandy said. "Lynching provides a big-time social gathering. Wagons and buggies loaded with family and friends come in from all over Grimes County and beyond to attend these hangings. After the hangings, we have bands playing. Dancing and picnics are part of the show. Shopping is always brisk. Lines form for my ice cream. We don't want the town cleaned up too much. Hangings are good for the economy."

Kandy could tell we wanted more. She gave us two more whopping scoops of ice cream. Frank and I left eating our ice cream out of a cup.

We sat down on a park bench and continued our conversation.

"Delicious," Frank said. "Heard about it, but my first time for ice cream. I think I'll be going back there quite a bit."

The warm sun began melting my two scoops of vanilla. I spooned several bites into my mouth and wiped my lips with my bandana. "The merchants seem to think we have come here to rid the town of Negroes. There's a lot of misinformation going around town."

"There are two sides to every story," Frank said.

"Sometimes it's difficult to tell the good from the bad," I replied. "Take the outlaw Butch Cassidy, for example. They say that he was a real charmer, witty and handsome." I said.

"But not nearly as charming, witty, handsome, and intelligent as you and me," Frank said.

"Certainly not. We're magnets for women."

We sat there in silence, waiting for women to come running out of the buildings to smother us with hugs and kisses. None came.

Undaunted, I said, "I can understand why women drool for us, but why do some women seem to be enamored with bank robbers like Butch Cassidy and Sundance Kid? We're paragons of virtue," I said with a wink and a smile. "Butch and Sundance were outlaws."

"Some attractive and otherwise intelligent women fall for 'bad boys.' They provide a sense of adventure and wildness," Frank said. "Cassidy and Sundance had the aura of the outlaw-as-hero, western Robin Hoods who stole from the rich. People seek wealth, and at the same time, they often scorn the rich. They like to see the bad guys get away with bamboozling the wealthy; something that deep in their hearts they would like to do."

"You sound like Sigmund Freud." I grinned.

"Never heard of him," Frank replied.

"Just as well. He's another charlatan. He's got people in Europe believing that little girls want to have sex with their daddies. Writes and goes around speaking about what he calls psychoanalysis. Makes up stories about his patients and publishes them as case studies. I heard about him when I was at Yale. He's creating quite a brouhaha with the academics and upper crust."

"Academics will fall for anything. They have no common sense," Frank said with derision. "And the so-called upper crust are simply fad followers who can't think for themselves."

"Why do you have such difficulty expressing your emotions?" I quipped.

We stood, stretched, and, continued to tour the town, admiring the soaring Victorian homes and mansions along eastern Washington Street and nestling along the adjacent blocks. On the street south and parallel to Washington Street stood the churches—Methodist, Baptist, Presbyterian, Episcopal—with peaked roofs and tall steeples. The small Catholic Chapel a few streets down from the others rested modestly on a small lot.

"More churches than believers," I said.

"They build churches so hypocrites can feel good about themselves," Frank said. "These plantation owners—and really the normal citizens, too, the regular white folks—they ridicule, cuss, beat, and hang black people and then go to Baptist, Methodist, whatever church every Sunday."

"Do you reckon hypocrites don't know there're hypocrites?" I asked.

"Now that is a good question," Frank said. "I've often asked myself how these so-called Christians can go to church on Sunday and beat up the blacks on Monday. You were a preacher once. You tell me," Frank said.

"None of us can see our own faults," I said. "And we can't tell what's in another person's heart."

We sat on the steps of the First Baptist Church enjoying the shade of a magnificent red oak towering above the church steeple.

"When I was a kid growing up, my family went to church every Sunday," Frank said. "My mother was a Baptist; my father, a Methodist. One Sunday we would go to the Baptist church; the next Sunday to the Methodist. I favored the shorter Methodist services—two hoots and a holler and then it was time for lunch.

"John Wesley reigns supreme," I said.

Baptist sermons were longer than a 30-year mortgage. After a sermon bringing down hell fire and damnation interrupted by shouts of "Amen" and sometimes other words of approbation from the congregation, the choir would sing the invitation hymns "Just as I Am" or "I Surrender All," and the preacher, with fervent pleadings, would urge sinners to come forward and join the church. If no one came down, another verse would be sung ... and another ... and another until someone got so hungry, they would 'surrender all' to end the exhortations. After a full-fledged prayer by an elder, the congregation would file by and, with a handshake, welcome the new members into the fold. By that time, people were too weak to walk to lunch.

I chuckled. Two kids ran down the street kicking a can and giggling. A young lady in a colorful ankle-length dress pushed a perambulator holding an infant. The bouncing can startled her.

"Since Baptists believed that only complete immersion could accomplish baptism, they had ceremonies at a cattle tank or in the river," I said. "After Sam Houston joined the church, he was asked if his baptism in the Colorado River had washed away all his sins. 'If it did,' said old Sam, 'It killed all the fish down to the Gulf of Mexico.'"

We both laughed. The sun, hot in the cloudless sky, made me thankful for the cool shade of the oak. I picked up a small stick lying on the steps, broke it in two, and tossed the two sticks onto the church lawn.

"Denominations seem more interested in doctrine and dogma than Christian ethics and Christian living," Frank said.

"Denominations certainly have differences," I said. "Take the Episcopalians and their drinking, dancing, and loose living. They do in public what the other denominations do in private. The grim-faced, frozen-chosen Presbyterians believe they have been elected to go to heaven. If they know they are going to heaven, why do they brood and sulk? A joyful Presbyterian is an oxymoron. Catholics don't have to read; the priest will tell them what to believe. Lutherans dispute over the question of transubstantiation—whether the bread and wine of communion become the actual body and blood of Christ; and feelings run high on the subject. Why do snake-charming Pentecostals who preach faith healing die of rattlesnake bites? During a Methodist General Conference I attended, a layman stood up from his seat in the congregation and announced: 'A thousand years after Christianity is dead and forgotten, the Methodist Church will still be marching triumphantly forward.'"

Frank cackled, took off his hat, pulled a bandana out of his back pocket, wiped his forehead, and put his hat back on. He continued to hold the bandana in his left hand.

"The two largest protestant denominations are the Baptist and the Methodist," Frank said. "Though my family went to Methodist and Baptist churches indiscriminately, there were noticeable differences in emphasis. The Baptists were much more apt to stress the importance of coming forward to be saved: in fact, it is a tenant of their faith that 'once saved, always saved,' and it seemed that salvation went with baptism. When a Baptist is baptized, he comes away saying that he has been saved; when a Methodist is baptized—by sprinkling—he comes away saying that he has been put on probation pending good behavior. A Baptist who misbehaved was said to have backslid; when a Methodist misbehaves, he is said to have 'fallen from grace.'"

"I have always been much more comfortable with Methodist doctrine, which puts an emphasis on good works," I said. "The Baptists and the Methodist both believe that man is saved by the grace of God without any reference to the man's merits; man is only required to accept that grace. My grandfather's favorite Bible verse was Micah 6:8: 'What doth the Lord require of thee, but to do justly, and to love mercy, and to walk humbly with God?' My grandfather, grandmother and father believed that another key verse in the Bible was John 3:16 'For God so loved the world, that he gave his only begotten son, that whosoever believeth in him should not perish, but have everlasting life.'"

"That verse is Christianity in a nutshell," Frank said. "If we confess our sins, believe that Jesus has been sent by God to save us from our sins, and live a life worthy of the Lord, we are Christians."

"All the rest is wasteful theology, silly doctrine, and restrictive dogma," I said.

Chapter 11

WITH OUR TRANSITION to Navasota, Frank had a pile of paperwork to complete, so I walked over to the Emporium Hotel and Restaurant for a cup of coffee. I wanted to get the lay of the land. I've found that bored bartenders, chatty nurses, and gossipy waitresses have more valuable news than the *Farmer's Almanac*.

A woman who looked to be a little past middle age with a jaunty step and a welcoming smile put down her newspaper and poured me a cup of coffee as soon as I sat down. Her black hair with a bluish tinge and the aquiline bridge of the nose seemed incompatible with her fair skin and a few scattered freckles. Her chatter was certainly more Irish than Indian.

"Deputy McAbee, I'm glad you and Ranger Hamer have arrived. I know that Gladys Shine wrote Governor Campbell, but I didn't know he would send the top Rangers in Texas."

"We just got here. How can you know all this?"

"Information is my entertainment. I've been a waitress here before Moses was put in a basket. I have ears bigger than my mouth. Good talkers have to be good listeners."

I motioned for her to sit down. She sat and put the coffee pot on the table. "I'm Mildred Baer," she said. "That's spelled B-A-E-R. My husband was a full-blood German. Soon after our marriage, he left for a hunting trip in Colorado. When he was skinning an elk, a grizzly smelled blood, and killed him for the meat. I've been a waitress ever since." Mildred paused for a beat, and then said, "That was a long time ago. I've adjusted. I tell people that a Baer was killed by a bear."

"Ironic," I said.

"People say I could talk the legs off a chair and a gate off its hinges, but I do stop for an oiling now and then."

She gave me another wink. She knew she was a gossip and was proud of it.

"This restaurant is practically my home," she said. "I'm here from opening to closing. I chase news like a fox hunts for a hole. I can hear a whisper in a whirlwind. If it's happening, I know it. Heck fire, sometimes I know it before it happens."

I began to learn that Mildred had a cavernous mind; her mouth was an open portal to a prodigious amount of information—some of it valuable, a good deal of it true, and all of it laced with enough hokum to wake up a committee. I had a feeling that she could weave facts with fiction so well that I wouldn't be able to tell where the truth ended and the legend began.

"I amuse people with my gossip, but I know when to rest my tongue and when to wear it out. Knowing when to shut up and when to talk increases my tips." As if to demonstrate her point, Mildred launched into a flibbertigibbet about Gladys Shine: "Gladys has a way of getting her way. She went after that Weaver boy, Zack Weaver's son. They own that huge apiary down in Lynn Grove. They sell gallons of honey all around these parts and ship queen bees and package bees up north every spring. They breed queen bees like ranchers breed cattle."

I took a sip of coffee and looked around the room. Why did I need to know all this?

"Now Gladys has more money than she can say grace over what with her dad getting rich in the railroad business. Good business to get into. Sure is. Now Roy—that's Zack's son—he has a law degree from the University of Texas and an entomology degree from Texas A&M."

Yes Sir! *She knows her town*, I thought. We'll need a sifter as big as Blunderbore's to filter the minutia from the important stuff. Editor Clemons ought to plug her into the printing press and let her rip. If he could print her words the way she said them, he would sell out the *Navasota Examiner Review* every week.

"Gladys is ... uhh ... emotional ... dramatic. She sometimes acts like a calf that lost its mama. She knows how to make a glass eye cry. She's daddy's little girl; that's as certain as Annie Oakley hitting her mark ... but she is bright as a penny. And she adores brainy people. So she jumped on Roy like a duck on a June bug. I wonder how that marriage is going to work. She's allergic to bees."

Monty is a mute compared to Mildred, I thought.

"They have a wedding coming next month, and it's not soon enough if you ask me. They'll be having a seven-month baby, or I don't know a widget from a whangdoodle. Anyway, Gladys found a dasher for her churn, if you know what I'm talking about."

I laughed. Mildred leaned toward me.

"I just want you to know you can count on Gladys for support ... her father too ... and the Weavers. They all are disgusted at the way the coloreds are treated around here. The Weavers pay their coloreds white man's wages. This doesn't sit well with the Ku Klux Klan."

That was a long wind-up before the pitch, I thought. *But very, very interesting— and helpful. Frank will be fascinated.*

Her eyes met mine. She leaned close enough to me that I got a whiff of kitchen grease and lavender soap. She lowered her voice almost to a whisper. "I can tell you everything—I mean everything about this town. I know you are here to stop Spurger, and Spurger will do anything he can to drive you away."

Mildred paused, looked around. No one had entered the restaurant. She moved her chair closer to mine.

"I hate Spurger," she said. "My mother was a full blood Comanche. When the railroads were built, hunters killed all the buffalo. She almost starved. She moved with her tribe from place to place with the U.S Army in pursuit. They were herded like cattle into an Oklahoma reservation. She died when a drunken army sergeant hit her over the head with the butt of his gun. Spurger treats Negros worse than the army treated my mother. I will help you take Spurger down any way I can."

Chapter 12

I WAS MAKING A FRESH pot of coffee. Frank was reading a story in the newspaper about us coming into town.

"It didn't take Clemens long to print up the news about us. He got the facts straight mostly, with a few stretches here and there," Frank was saying when we heard a ruckus outside.

I grabbed my shotgun, and we stepped out on the porch to investigate.

It was the first time that I saw a Texas Aggie as they called them. He looked normal but acted awful strange. I found out later that his name was Will H. Brown. In 1880, he was in the first graduating class of the Agricultural and Mechanical College of Texas—and mighty proud of it.

His father had bought up all the small farms around Milligan just north of Navasota when the Yellow Fever epidemic hit in 1872, and he turned those little pieces of land into a huge plantation. After his father died, Will became patriarch of one of the twelve aristocratic families who practically ran the town of Navasota. Will thought he was a big shot and could get away with just about anything.

There we were standing on the jailhouse porch looking down on Will H. Brown and a passel of cronies and onlookers. Brown wore a nicely pressed suit and a derby hat. He had a rather longish, well-trimmed gray beard that failed to cover a cocky smile on his face. His hands were on his hips with his arms akimbo making him look like the rooster he thought he was. Suddenly he tipped his head back and let out an ear-piercing, high pitched wail that rattled the jailhouse windows and started the dogs howling.

Frank stepped down from the porch and walked up to Brown, who was still wailing. Frank stood there until Brown was out of breath and then said, "I guess you know that I am Frank Hamer the new City Marshal. But you must not know about the new Navasota City Rules my deputy and I posted all over town. That big man standing on the porch with the sawed down shotgun is my deputy, Jude McAbee."

"Howdy," I said as I nodded toward the crowd, the shotgun cradled in the crook of my left arm.

"One of the new rules is about disturbing the peace," Frank said.

"I ain't disturbin' the peace. I'm just practicin' my Aggie yell for the upcomin' football game," Brown said with that cocky grin still on his face.

They must not teach grammar at A&M, I thought.

"I'm the one who decides about disturbing the peace," Frank said congenially like he was talking to a good neighbor, "and I say you're disturbing it. I'll let it go this time on account of you're not having read the new rules yet."

The crowd stirred a little, but no one protested. A few snickered.

Frank tipped his hat toward them and said, "Nice to see all of you. I hope to get around and meet most of y'all personal sometime soon." He turned, and we both walked into the jail.

Before we could sit down, here comes another high-pitched wail. We both walked out the door. I stayed on the porch. Frank meandered down the porch steps easy-like, as if he were going fishing on sleepy summer morning. He strolled up to Brown.

Suddenly, and as quick as a snake strike, he grabbed a handful of Brown's gray beard with his right hand, put his left foot out, bent his knee, and flipped Brown over his thigh onto the dusty street.

Brown had his breath knocked out of him and was gasping for air when Frank started kicking him in the direction of the jail. Brown began crawling on his hands and knees. Frank kicked him all the way up the jailhouse steps and to the door and then said, "Get up off your knees and walk into that cell. I'm tired of kicking you."

I remained out on the porch watching the crowd. When Brown and Frank got to the jailhouse door, the crowd vanished as quickly as a jackrabbit pursued by a hound dog. I stood there for a while watching them disappear into buildings up and down the street.

When all was settled and quiet, I opened the jailhouse door and entered the office. Frank was leaning back in his chair with his feet on the office desk, sipping his coffee. Brown, locked in his cell and rubbing his backside, moaned and groaned that he needed to see a doctor. I picked up my coffee cup. The coffee was still hot.

"We have our first jailbird," Frank said. "An Aggie"

"Hook 'em," I said.

Chapter 13

FRANK AND I WERE making our rounds through the streets enjoying the washed air that came from the thundering rainstorm that had just blown through the town. Light from the pale streetlights flickered on the wet street. We hadn't taken more than a few steps when we heard yelling a few blocks up the street. The streetlights and the red setting sun allowed us to make out two men dragging a black man to the back of a two-mule wagon where they quickly wrapped a rope around the man's chest, knotted it, and tied the dangling end to the back of the wagon.

The men climbed in the wagon. The man on the right side of the wagon seat grabbed the reins and with a "haw-up," the mules began pulling the wagon. The tied man tried to keep pace with the mules, but he stumbled and fell. The mules and wagon kept moving forward, dragging the man tied behind. A crowd of men followed. I couldn't make out how many.

Immediately, Frank ran into the street and waved his arms, commanding the wagon to stop. The wagon kept coming at an ever-increasing pace. Frank pulled his Colt and shot the lead mule in the head. The mule fell thunderously, canting the wagon to the left.

Both men sitting in the wagon seat yelled obscenities at Frank.

"You shot my mule," the man still holding the reins yelled. "That's a valuable animal you just kilt. You can't do that. Go around shooting mules like that. That's a trained mule. You are going to pay for this. You owe me $500 dollars for that trained mule."

Frank casually took the spent shell out of the chamber and replaced it with a cartridge from his belt. "That mule is not near as valuable as that man you're pulling behind the wagon."

"That's not a man. That's a nigger," the passenger yelled.

"He touched a white woman on the arm. That's a hangin' offense. We're taking him down the street to hang him off that oak tree up yonder," the driver said.

Both men got out of the wagon. One carried an ax handle; the driver reached for a shotgun. Frank fired. The shotgun flew out of the driver's hand. He went to his knees, blood gushing from his hand. He yelled obscenities between groans and moans.

"Hold 'em here," Frank said paying no attention to the cussing and shouting. He walked to the back of the wagon.

I stepped out on the street and racked my takedown. Ka-Chung! With that sound, the crowd stepped back. "Best for your health to drop that ax handle," I said to the passenger as I brought the takedown to my shoulder.

I don't know if my encouraging words or my shotgun influenced him the most. No matter. He dropped the ax handle right quick. A faint smell of sour beer came from both men.

The men following the wagon began gathering around the wounded driver. One of the bystanders handed the bleeding man a bandana. I watched carefully for anyone who might take offense for what just happened.

"All right get back a little ways," I said. "I'll blast anyone who makes a move for a gun."

The crowd seemed stunned. "You got a new sheriff and deputy in town. Things are changing. I won't mind shooting anyone who tries to make trouble."

The crowd stirred a little. They began to grumble. I could tell they didn't like us taking the side of a black man.

"Show's over, men. You can get off the street now." I pivoted my shotgun toward them.

The disgruntled men began to move off the street rather reluctantly. I steered the wagon driver and passenger toward the jail. The driver tried to staunch the blood oozing around his hand, which dangled grotesquely from his wrist. His face was blanched. He winced in pain. He groaned obscenities.

The passenger doubled his fist and stared menacingly at me. For a brief second, I thought he was going to leap toward me. He wasn't that stupid. He stood unclenching and clenching his fists.

I nudged him with my shotgun. "Help your buddy get to the jailhouse. The quicker he gets there, the faster he gets medical treatment."

They both turned and headed that way.

Out of the corner of my eye, I saw Frank struggling to untie the twisted rope from around the man's chest. I looked again. He wasn't a grown man. He had the slim build of a boy growing into manhood. The boy was frightened and confused.

The boy babbled, "Please don't hurt me sir. I didn't mean to brush up to that nice woman, sir. Please don't whip me, sir." Then he passed out.

As Frank headed to the doc across the street cradling the young man in his arms, he looked at the dead mule. "Got 'em square in the head," he said to no one in particular: "They say a mule is as hardheaded as a beer-brewing German woman, but that one wasn't hardheaded enough to stop a .45 slug."

After I locked the wounded man's buddy in a cell, I took the driver to the sink and began washing the wound. I dried the hand with a towel and compressed the towel around the wound until the oozing stopped. I wrapped the hand with gauze. I gave the man a glass of water that he gulped down. His color improved. I locked him in the cell next to his partner who was sound asleep, snoring loudly.

Chapter 14

WHEN I JOINED FRANK at the doctor's office, no one noticed me standing in the doorway. The boy had been washed. He had a towel around his waist. His cuts and scrapes had been doctored with a purplish liquid that emitted a sharp, clean smell.

The unconscious boy lay on the examining table, bruised and battered, abrasions over most of his body. The doc was examining him for broken bones when the boy's eyes opened and then closed again. I stepped in the room. The doc looked up with a puzzled smile. He had a full head of unruly black hair. The fine wrinkles on his cheeks and around his mouth and the inelastic, thin facial skin reflected a heavy smoker.

When he saw my badge, he motioned me over toward Frank who stood in the corner of the room, watching the doctor intently. "I'm Leonard Coleman," he said. "My hands are a little too bloody for shaking. I knew you boys were in town and figured you'd be over here sooner rather than later. I hope you can do something about this town. Things like this keep me busier than a hound dog in a forest of raccoons."

The boy opened his eyes, stirred some.

"Mance, I'm Dr. Coleman do you remember me?" The boy nodded his head affirmatively. "You are in my office; just rest easy," the doctor said. "You are going to be fine in a few days."

I let out an audible sigh. The boy was so fragile looking. Then I got mad. Real mad. We should string those two thugs from the nearest tree.

The boy looked around the room, closed his eyes, and immediately fell to sleep. We left the sleeping boy and walked into the next room.

"Mance,' I whispered. "Never heard that name before."

"Short for Emancipation," the doctor said as he began putting his instruments back in place. "I've known the family for a long time. I treat them when they are sick. Mance is almost famous around Grimes County. Just about everyone knows about his awesome guitar style. I have never heard one person make such resonant music come from one guitar. If you close your eyes and listen, you think there are several guitars playing. And he sings too in a thick East Texas black accent."

"Is he going to recover?" I asked. "Will he be able to play again?"

"He'll be fine. Big bruise on his head, but no permanent damage; no bones broken; fingers and hands have small cuts, but no real damage; bruises and lacerations—they'll all heal fairly quickly, one of the many blessings of the young. He should be back playing that guitar soon."

"Amazing that a boy could be dragged like that and have no major damage," I said.

"There's a small chance he could develop a subdural hematoma—a bruise on the brain—from that blow on the head. I'd like to keep him here overnight, just to be certain nothing untoward happens."

"You certainly seem to know what you are doing a lot more than those sawbones in the Trans-Pecos," I said.

All the while Frank stood by fuming. His face was as red as a whore's lipstick. He kept opening and closing his fists, gazing at the wall.

"Been doctors in my family ever since 1789," Dr. Coleman said. "My father didn't have more training than turkeys in the rain, but he had common sense and learned by doing. That's the way all of us doctors out here on the prairie learn—by doing. We're practicing."

"You practiced up pretty good, Doc," I said.

"My daddy told me that when you hear hoof beats think of horses, not zebras. Always look for the most common explanation. You can learn a lot by simply listening to the patient and by smelling. Measles smell like fresh plucked feathers; scarlet fever smells like hot bread; diphtheria smells like rotting apples. Sugar diabetes has a fruity smell. Kidney failure smells like ammonia. Patients with liver disease have a musty odor. Foul smelling sputum suggests a lung abscess. Are y'all hungry? Let's go over to the Emporium and get something to eat."

"Yuck," I said. "You just talked about all these sickening smells, and now you want to eat."

Dr. Coleman chuckled and began scribbling in a notebook. "I'll call my nurse to keep an eye on Mance. After dinner, I will check on him ... oh, and venereal disease smells like stale beer."

I didn't know whether to slug the doc or laugh. I wondered what disease smelled like whiskey, but I surely didn't ask him.

Chapter 15

IT WAS LATE WHEN WE finished dinner. Frank and Dr. Coleman left. I hung around drinking coffee. It wasn't long before the last customers—a young man with a woman clinging to his arm—left. Mildred came over. She pointed to a side door of the restaurant.

"Spurger was having dinner with a few cronies in that private room tonight. I was their waitress. I always wait on Spurger. He thinks I like him, and because of that, he likes me. When the hubbub on the street began, Spurger stood by the window and watched the whole thing. He became more and more upset. He had been drinking heavily. The whiskey inflamed his rage. He began ranting about Governor Campbell. His friends tried to calm him, but then he launched into Captain Rogers. 'You'd think the great Texas Rangers would want to protect us, but no they're here to harass us, to prevent us from taking care of the nigger problem. I will take care of Hamer and McAbee. I'll find some way. It will have to be a good plan—a plan that will make me Governor Campbell's best friend,'" he said.

Mildred paused and looked out the window. The streets were empty.

"What a slimy creep of a worm," she said.

"Worm. No. He's more like the Gaboon viper that dwells in the deepest, darkest jungles of the Congo. The huge Gaboon viper is about as long as you are tall with a width as big as your arm. The large and triangular head has a pair of horns protruding between its nostrils. The Gaboon's multicolored scales blend in with dry leaves. Lying in camouflage, the viper hunts by ambush, striking with blinding speed, much faster than a rattlesnake. The two-inch fangs hold on to the victim, injecting ounce after ounce of venom. The deadly venom causes nerve damage and keeps the blood from clotting. The victim falls to the ground defenseless, losing bowel and bladder control. As the Gaboon's bite sinks deeper and deeper, the skin blisters and rots. The victim cries bloody tears of agony. An ugly death comes quickly. Yes, Spurger is like the Gaboon viper— destroying anything that gets in his way."

Mildred turned as pale as a bucket of milk. Her hands shook so when she poured me coffee, half of it splattered on the table. "You better stop messing with that Mexican mistress of his. If Spurger finds out, he will strike as fast as the Gaboon viper."

"How ... do you know about us?"

"This Baer never hibernates," she said.

After a pause, I asked Mildred to pass a note to her.

"You have an immunity to Gaboon bites?" Mildred asked. "And what about the girl? You are putting her in danger. Actually, she's not a Mexican. She's a half-breed: Comanche daddy; Mexican mother; raised as a Comanche. She likes to call herself Stardust from her Indian name, *She Who Dusts the Heavens with Bright Stars*. Spurger calls her Maria. He treats her worse than a slave."

"I'll figure a way to rescue her," I said. "I'll never get to see her alone. I want her to know that I'm smitten by her. If she feels the same, I can work out an escape plan."

Mildred was reluctant at first, but I kept after her until she agreed to pass notes if she found times that were perfectly safe to do so.

"Spurger is a monster,' she said. "We've got to be awfully careful."

Chapter 16

MANCE WAS SITTING UP and dressed when we saw him the early the next morning. Because the colored weren't allowed to eat at a white man's restaurant, we ordered some breakfast for the three of us at the Emporium and had breakfast at the jailhouse office.

Mance downed three scrambled eggs, several pieces of bacon, two biscuits heavy with gravy, and five pancakes. Frank and I sat there watching, amazed at the young man's prodigious appetite. He began telling us about his life on the plantation:

"All my family, my mama and pa and eleven of us kids work on Allenfawm—that's Mista Spurger's plantation; Allenfawm is the most hugest plantation of 'em all," Mance said.

I had heard about Allen farm. It stretched for 15,000 acres over the Brazos River bottom. It had a post office, three-story depot, and three saloons. Over a hundred Negro workers and their families lived on the farm. They were paid in Allen farm tokens where they could buy groceries at the company store and commissary.

"We never seen Mista Spurger much and plenty glad that we don't.' He come out on the fields ever' onest in a while but he lets the big boss man Mista Tom Landis run the show. Mista Tom is a bad man. Worser than any other man. He whip ya for nothin.' I wrote a song about him. Call it 'Tom

Landis' Farm.' I'm real careful where I sing it though on account Mista Tom liable to kill me if he knowd I wrote it. The big boss man, Mista Tom sho' does work you too. Mista Tom has a big 'ole bell.

"At five o'clock the bell ring. This bell means get to the lot, git ya mule an git his hawness on 'em an git to the fields. If ya not in that lot by 5 o'clock ya git a lashin that brings blood. Whip women too and little chillin.

"They don't have to ring no bell fur us ta come out at night, cause we can't quit 'til the sun go down: that's can't to can't. Can't see, to can't see."

"The Civil War ended 50-years ago ... nothing has changed," Frank said.

"This is the worser thang I never seed," Mance continued. "Enoch has a wife Hattie. She fall down in the field, sick. Enoch, he picks her up. He takin her back toward the house. Mista Tom rode the hawss up to Enoch. Enoch say Mista Tom I'm goin to help Hattie get home. She sick.

"Mista Tom ride the hawss in front of him. Enoch caught holt of the hawse's reins ta keep the hawss from steppin on im. Pushed the hawss away with the reins. Mista Tom took out a pistol an shot em in the neck the first lick. With the next one he hit 'em right in the heart. Enoch, he fall—thud—dead."

"The more things change, the more they remain the same," I said.

"Nothing has changed," Frank said.

"About a hunnud of us niggers gathered around. I nudged up front where I could see everythang. Mista Spurger he come ridin' up fast from the house. He jump off from that hawss. Mista Tom he says 'Enoch started up on me wit a knife. I shot em because he was aimin' to kill me with that knife.' I don't see no knife. Hunnud niggers standin there they don't see no knife.

"Mista Spurger comes over. He kneels down beside Enoch. I'm right there where I can see. Mista Spurger he pull a knife out of his pocket. Lay it down right there ... sort of under Enoch's body."

Frank and I didn't say anything. We just looked at each other.

"The hot son was makin Enoch swell up. The womens they kiverted em up wit a old blanket."

"If nobody had seen the shooting, Spurger would have had the corpse dumped in the Navasota River," Frank said.

"They sent for the law. Sheriff Maker he come out. So Sheriff Maker askt Mista Tom what happin. Mista Tom, he say, 'Enoch stawted up on me, wit a knife. I shot im cause I didn want im ta cut me with his knife.'

"Sherriff Maker, he says, 'Well, where is the knife at?'

"Mista Spurger say, 'I found it right under his body and I left it where I found it. Lift up that blanket an look at that awm that's under his back an yu see it there.'

"Sherriff Maker, he don't askt no questions. You know there wuz over a hunnud people standin there. Didn ask one of im no questions. I knowd what happin, but too scared to say. So they passed it o' Enoch havin a knife. Mista Tom didn go ta jail. An didn pay no fine. So when they kilt a colored man on a fawm, the'd say anythang an git by. You know they have a little go-by, they say, 'Kill a mule, buy anothuh. Kill a nigger hire anothuh.'

"Nawsuh! Navasota jailhouse built fur us niggers. White folks git away with anythang. Them big bankers; them big landowners; them big store owners they turn it over to Mista Spurger. He make the law. An he get that Klu Kluck to hep em. All Mista Spurger's men, they go out scarin the people that don't have the mind what Mista Spurger got."

"You aren't going back to that farm," Frank said real tender-like. "You're going to be my aid. You'll drive me around the plantations and farms in the buggy, open fences for me, set up targets for me to practice shooting, and such. We're going to inspect those farms and plantations and make sure the bosses are treating the workers right."

"No I can't do that. Mista Tom he still run that fahm. Mista Spurger his boss, but Mista Tom he big boss man on that fahm," Mance said. "Mista Tom— he'd cut off one of my nuts, and then he whup me til his arm wore out." Mance had a terrified look on his face. "You cross Mista Tom, he cross you out."

"I'll take care of Landis," Frank said. He had a cold, jump-out-of-the-way look.

Chapter 17

LUXURIOUS GREEN ST AUGUSTINE grass covered the courthouse lawn. Mance and I sat under a majestic red oak that provided a glorious summer shade. Mance played his guitar and sang. He was the best guitar player I had ever heard, and he was only 16. He called himself a songster. He could sing and play them all—ballads, rags, spirituals, all sorts of dance pieces, breakdowns, waltzes, just about anything I'd ask for.

"Music ain't no count if you don't put no season to it," he said. "Jest like a cook; if she come out here an don't have no salt in the bread, somebody ganna find out. Didn have no pepper in the meat. It's tasteless food. But as long as she kin cook wit a season to it, why that's a good cook. Well you got ta have a season ta this music. Jest like a cook. Then ta people git some vibration outa the music. It make thangs roll across their mind. These verses played right and sang right reach ya heart and reach yo mind."

Life is fine sitting under the shade of an oak tree with the wind blowing just enough to cool you, but not strong enough to irritate you while listening to a 16-year old raconteur weave tales as easily as he played the guitar.

"Sometimes I sing this song; this heart song 'bout my friend that done got hanged. I wrote it so it will break your heart when you hear it. I call it a True Story Song, a break your heart song."

Mance told me this story:

A 15-year-old friend of his, Tommy Jim, started seeing a white girl in Navasota. They soon began making love. Sometimes he would visit her in her bedroom. One night, he got careless and stayed too long. In a rush, he knocked over a garbage can. The noise woke everybody up, but Tommy Jim was too fast for the papa, and he got away.

The papa rounded up thirty or forty white men who got on his trail carrying guns and riding horses with dogs howling and yelping as they followed Tommy Jim's scent. They caught him in the willow thickets on the bank of the Brazos River. They let the dogs attack him for a long while. Finally, they threw him on a horse and took him to jail.

The girl confessed to the family what she and Tommy Jim had been doing all along. All the family got together and told her to never tell anyone about the affair.

The girl's family was very poor, but they wanted to press charges against Tommy Jim. They told Robert Spurger what happened, and he gave the judge $1000 to hush her disgrace. The papa testified that Tommy Jim was robbing the house when he saw his daughter sleeping in her bed and raped her. The judge did not allow Tommy Jim or the girl to testify. They hung Tommy Jim right there in the jailhouse.

When he finished the story, Mance said, "That makes for a True Story Song that twists ya heart so tight that when I play and sing it all the peoples say 'hush. Don't play that song everbody cryin.'"

Mance looked down and wiped his eyes.

When he became composed, he said, "You know what? When I play and sang that song when I'm all by myself practicin' most of the time I can't hardly finish it neither. It makes me cry. Ever time I play it, I cry. I think of my friend, poor Tommy Jim and I cry. That's a heart song, a True Story Heart Song." Mance began strumming, "Motherless Children," a haunting, melodious song. "If God loves us, why does God let so many bad people live in this world?" he asked, his fingers flying over the frets.

"That is a fantastic question Mance. When I preached and Baptized, do you know the most frequent question I got from people?"

"Probably somethang like why does God let evil in this world. Or why does a loving God let bad things to happen. Somethang like that."

"Yes, Mance, 'Why does a lovin' God allow bad thangs?' I have done hours of studying and praying over this question. There is no short answer to this question. It's a long answer. When I start talking, you might think you are in the Baptist Church hungry for lunchtime. You might go to sleep with my longwinded explanation."

"Go ahead, Mista Jude. I'll just listen and play while you're talkin.'"

Mance began playing, 'Trouble in Mind.' I tried to make my explanation as simple as I could. Theologians wouldn't like my explanation, but I don't give a damn. I was talking to Mance, not academics.

"God's plan is to help us become more spiritual—to grow closer to him. He does this by testing us. It's sort of like when we go to school; we are tested to see if we learned what we should. God grades our papers. God appointed Lucifer—'the light bearer'—to be the head master teacher. By and by, Lucifer began to think he was hot stuff, and decided he didn't need God. He called himself Satan. Satan means adversary or opponent or rival or competitor. Satan found a bunch of bad teachers and called them devils. Devil means, 'to oppose.' Satan and his devils left heaven and set up camp on earth. Satan and the devils work to turn us humans against God. When humans choose to join Satan, God is sad. The more people Satan can turn against God, the prouder and more rebellious Satan gets.

"Now why didn't God wipe out Satan and all the devils? Answer: God gave Satan, his devils, and God's people—us—the power to choose. God gives us the power to love him. If God does not give us the power to choose, our love for God would be false love.

"God gave us free will. If God didn't give us free will, we would be puppets. Puppets are wooden. Puppets have no heart. Puppets cannot love. Puppets cannot choose. Because God gave us free will, God must stand by and let us make choices. God hates evil, but God has decided not to interfere. God has decided not to punish. We punish ourselves by the choices we make. Evil exists because God allows evil to exist. Without the temptation of evil, we cannot choose the love of God.

"God sent us Jesus to save us from our sins. When we choose to surrender our lives to the love of Jesus, God will save us from the power of Satan. God also sent us the Holy Spirit to guide us—to set our minds on what God desires for us. The soft, gentle voice of the Holy Spirit gives us hope in God all the daylong.

"Because of his overweening pride, Spurger has chosen to reject God's way and join Satan and his minions. Power and wealth made Spurger believe he didn't need God. He uses evil ways to bring him more power and wealth.

"What I'm going to say sounds awfully sentimental, but I'm no poet. I'm no wordsmith. I can only tell what I am thinking. I can only tell what I feel in my heart. Frank and I have chosen the better path—to help the outcast when nobody else can—to help the poor and downtrodden, the abused and the neglected. God will show us the way. We fear no evil because God is our shield."

All the time I had been talking, Mance had been finger picking his guitar. He didn't say anything after I finished my long-winded talk. I stretched my legs. He began to sing, "Amazing Grace."

Chapter 18

MANCE WAS SINGING, "You Got to Reap What You Sow" when Frank joined us. He had been at the barbershop for a 10-cent shave and a haircut. Just about the time Frank was about to sit down under the oak with us, a man with a pearl-handle Colt resting in a low slug holster swaggered toward us. The holster strapped to his right thigh gave him the recognizable gunslinger look. His angular face, narrow nose, and greasy black hair that hung down to his shoulders reminded me of an Indian, maybe a half-breed. A rawhide quirt was strapped to his left wrist.

"Mr. Spurger wants that nigger back on the plantation. He sent me to fetch him," the gunslinger said.

Frank turned his full body to the half-breed. "I'm a little hard of hearing at times. Can you repeat that?"

"Mr. Spurger wants that nigger boy back on the plantation."

"Can't file a claim on this boy," Frank said. "He's working for me now. He drives me around and opens gates for me. Drives my buggy around when I'm collecting guns from households with a bad reputation."

"That nigger belongs to Mr. Spurger."

"He never did, and he never will," Frank said, and his pupils constricted.

I've seen that same grin on Frank's face spook many a man. I can almost hear them say to themselves, 'We are about to get in a drawdown and

Hamer is smiling at me. He doesn't seem worried. Maybe he is as good as people say. Maybe he is better than me. Maybe I should let it go and walk away—alive.'

I could tell by the way the gunslinger stood, slightly crouched, the way he held his hand next to his Colt. He was trying to decide: can I beat Hamer? Should I try?

"You think you can outdraw me?" he asked trying to talk himself into going for his gun.

"I'm not sure," Frank said. "So far, I've been fast enough, but you never can tell. This might be your lucky day." Frank shrugged his shoulders nonchalantly and smiled.

The man was silent for a moment. His hand hovered over the Colt. The right side of his mouth twitched. He looked down. I could tell he had decided against going for his gun. His hands relaxed. His shoulders slumped slightly.

"I'll tell Mr. Spurger what you said ... and then we'll see."

"I haven't seen you around town before, so you must be new. Perhaps you haven't had time to read the city rules posted around. You might be particularly interested in the rule that says it's illegal to carry guns inside the city limits. If you are carrying the next time I see you, I'll have to take your weapon and lock you up for a couple of days," Frank said, relaxed and friendly like he was talking to his next-door neighbor.

The half-breed opened his mouth as if to say something; then he closed it. He stood looking Frank in the eye. He averted his eyes and said, "After I talk to Mr. Spurger, I'll be back."

As the man turned to walk away Frank said, "Don't forget to leave your guns at home."

The man flinched, stopped walking, and looked as if he were going to wheel around and face Frank. Instead, he walked away.

"Can you beat em, Mista Frank?" Mance asked.

"I never know until it's over," Frank said.

"I thought that we were going to have a real, bona fide dime novel shootout," I said.

"You need to improve your book selection," Frank said.

"He'll go to Spurger and figure a way to get us. Trouble is coming, but not today," I said. "A letter to Governor Campbell won't work because we are doing exactly what the governor wants."

"Yes," Frank said. "Trouble is coming. It always does when you are doing good. When evil attacks us, it means we are doing something right. Yes, trouble is coming. Maybe we ought to study up on some of your dime novels to see what to do."

I shrugged and grinned. "Sit for a while," I said to Frank. "This shady oak will cool you off. I was about to ask Mance about how he learned to play so well at an early age," I said.

Frank sat. He crossed his legs Indian style and leaned against the big trunk. He tipped his hat down over his eyes. "Well go on then."

I looked at Mance. His eyes were wide open; his pupils dilated; sweat was on his upper lip. I could see his heart pounding under his shirt. "Relax Mance," I said. "Marshal Hamer can take care of himself. You've seen him shoot. Everybody has heard about what he can do. Only a fool would try to outdraw him."

"This town is overstocked with fools," Frank said.

Chapter 19

JIMMY LEE KEPT OWLS and parrots on display in a large cage in his saloon. Frank liked to watch the owls and talk to the parrots. He especially enjoyed teaching new words to a blue-and-gold macaw that he called Sir Isaac Newton. He got a kick out of walking around the cage and watching the owls' heads swivel to keep up with his movements.

"Look at that big horned owl," he said to me. "Looks like he weighs ten pounds, but he is mostly feathers. Take away the thick feathers and he would weigh maybe 3 pounds. He has huge eyes. Look at those eyes. They are enormous compared to the rest of the head. That owl's eyeball weighs more than my eyeball. That's a heavy eye for a little owl. He surely looks smart with those big eyes. What do you think, Jude, are owls smart?"

"Well I guess they are. As they say, 'Wise as an owl.'"

"Nope. Owls are dumber than mildewed hay. They can't be trained to do the simplest tasks. These parrots here can talk. This macaw, I call him Newton, has a vocabulary of over three dozen words that I've counted so far. Hawks can be taught to retrieve objects. Pigeons can be used as messengers. You can't teach an owl squat."

Jimmy, who had been washing glasses, moved down to the end of the bar that was closest to the birdcage. "They sure are good hunters though. 85% kill rate I read somewhere."

"You're right," Frank said. "Those eyes enable them to do what God intended for them to do. Kill and eat, but because most of the owl's brain is made for vision, the thinking part of the brain is teeny."

"Well if they can kill and eat, I guess they are as smart as they need to be," I said.

Frank ordered lemonade. I got a shot of whiskey. We sat down at a window table so we could watch what was going on outside.

"A person who can get practical things done is smart," I said.

A person who can use knowledge to create new things or to figure out things is smarter," Frank said.

"What makes a genius?" I asked.

"The only genius I know is the blue-and-gold macaw over there," Frank said pointing in the direction of the birdcage.

"He can say a bunch of words, but does he know the meaning of those words?

"Working' on it," Frank said with a shrug.

"I figure a genius is a person who can do something easy that the rest of us can't do at all," I said taking a small sip of my whiskey.

"Geniuses are born, not made," Frank said.

I glanced out the window to see a tiny boy attempting to get a large hoop to stand on edge. The boy may have been five or six years old, but he was so tiny he looked younger. The hoop fell. The boy stood it on edge. The hoop fell. The boy stood it up. Eventually he got the hoop to stand long enough to roll it a few feet with a stick he held in his hand. He kept at it. Soon he rolled the hoop down the boardwalk disappearing out of sight.

"Grinders may have us all beat," I said. "They grind away slowly, but intensely focused until they have completed a difficult task. '*Thou they be grinders, they be fierce,*'" I said.

"Must be Shakespeare, I recognize the highfalutin way of saying things," Frank said. He threw a peanut to the macaw. "My entire point with the owl thing was that we all can be fooled by appearances every day of every year," Frank said.

Was he reading my mind?

"And we can be sucked in by tradition and opinion," he continued. "We have believed owls were wise since the Greeks said they were almost 3000 years ago."

"I guess that's why you are a good investigator," I said. "You form your own opinions."

"Sherlock Holmes of Texas sitting right here beside you," Frank said.

"You wear a Stetson. He wears a deerstalker hat. He smokes a pipe. You roll your own. I'm a little concerned though," I said with a laugh remembering what Frank said about owls. "Your eyes are huge."

Robert Spurger walked into the saloon with Stardust and two thugs. Spurger was wearing a navy-blue suit. His suit jacket with wide lapels fit loosely over a vertical stripped shirt with a round collar. His red paisley silk scarf tie and hand-tooled black boots gave him a dandy appearance. When Spurger saw us, he walked over followed by his entourage. "He hovered over us like a black cloud filled with lightning bolts."

"Did you see that boy rolling that enormous hoop down the boardwalk causing people to stumble and scatter? He nearly knocked my woman on her deliciously and perfectly round butt. I want him arrested for disturbing the peace," Spurger said with a derisive smile.

I didn't know if his request was serious or was meant to provoke. I did know that I abhorred his remarks about Stardust ... and I knew that Spurger caused my slime meter to rise higher each time I met him.

Frank's steely gaze froze with disgust.

Spurger must have noticed. He attempted to be polite, but a smarmy attitude prevailed. "This beautiful young lady's given name is Maria Sanchez," he said. "I rescued her from a sordid life when I led a reform group to the Dallas east side where thieves, dealers, killers, strippers, and whores hang out. She was Dixie Dazzler when I saved her from the Frolic Club two years ago.

Yes, praise the Lord. I rescued Dixie Dazzler and gave her real name back. What a blessing to be part of such a devoted and fearless group of Christian reformers that would be brave enough to meet Satan's minions head-on."

Frank looked as disgusted as I was.

For a second or two, my eyes met Stardust's. She gave a very slight nod that told me Spurger's story wasn't true.

"I know the Lord has appointed me as her friend, mentor and yes savior ... savior here on this evil infested Earth," Spurger continued. "I had her baptized in the Brazos immediately. Since then, she has served me sweetly, meeting my pressing Christian needs each and every day."

My hands doubled into fists. I wanted to pummel Spurger. He was so captivated by his own pious lies, he didn't seem to notice my anger—or maybe he did. Maybe he was trying to get me angry. Maybe this encounter had been planned.

"I feel so blessed to have had a small part in turning a 'soiled' dove into a prayerful Baptist who sings like a sparrow in the First Baptist Church Choir each and every Sunday."

A *living Uriah Heep*, I thought. He oozes the oil of hypocrites.

Spurger continued on chameleon-like, "Maria is such a sweet person with a sweet name, but I call her Mine. Puts sizzle in the branding iron so to speak," he sneered.

Stardust flushed. Anger flashed in her eyes. She turned her head ever so slightly, warning me. She calmed herself and locked her hands together, allowing her arms to form a V-shape as they tapered in front of her. "My hands tightly knotted into fists turned my knuckles white.

"You seem upset Deputy McAbee. Maybe you have a special interest in this voluptuous lady," Spurger said.

Frank, with his right hand hovering over his Colt handle, locked eyes with Spurger until Spurger dropped his gaze. I turned my eyes on the two thugs. The stocky one looked ready to leap toward me. The gunslinger crouched slightly, his hand ready to draw.

Sir Newton suddenly croaked, "Wild Bill Hickok."

The standoff was broken.

"Let me introduce you to my aides," Spurger said as if nothing preternatural had occurred. He motioned to the stocky, barrel-chested thug with massive arms and tree-trunk legs. He had a 12-inch sheath with a knife handle protruding strapped to his left side; a smaller sheath with knife was stuck under his belt. As proud as a breeder whose stallion had won first place at the County Fair, Spurger introduced the bruiser as Pack Hardy. "He's quite strong, and they tell me he's good with a knife. He's come to protect me from the niggers and ruffians who want me dead."

"It's difficult for me to believe that anyone would want to harm such a kind and generous Christian like you," I said, with a little too much scorn in the tone of my voice.

"The Lord has always protected me. I attend the First Presbyterian Church. God protects his elect," Spurger said ignoring my sarcasm.

"The elect aren't assured they'll live a life free of missteps," I said. "Life is less predictable than when a mule will crap. It's good to watch your step."

"Your comments are as inerrant as the Bible," Spurger countered, his lips curled into a snarl. "That's why I have two guardian angels to watch over me. Recently there's been a lot of ... can I say ... crap messing things up in my town, and I want it cleaned up. But I'm certain I won't need them because I know God will answer my fervent prayers to keep my town free of nigger lovers."

I glanced at Frank who placed both of his palms flat on the table. He had leaned forward slightly. At the same time, he appeared perfectly relaxed. He tapped his fingers on the table and then leaned back in the chair. "Please formally introduce us to your other guardian angel," he said with sarcasm in his voice. "We've met, but we didn't get his name."

Spurger introduced the taller, rawboned man as Whip Wilson.

Frank nodded. His face showed no expression.

"I told Whip here that the boy was a worthless nigger, not worth fighting over. Just so you know, Whip has a reputation of being the fastest draw east of the Pecos," Spurger said. "Brought him in for protection against any gunslinger who may come to town with menace in his heart. And if there is a fast gun already here, I figure Whip is my man."

Spurger nodded the bruisers toward the bar. He motioned toward Stardust, and she brought him a bottle of whiskey and a glass. She stood two steps behind and to the right of Spurger. She gave me a quick smile.

Spurger gulped two quick drinks, filled the shot glass a third time, and placed it on the table in front of him.

"Lemonade?" Spurger said to Frank.

"On duty," Frank said. He paused looking at the full glass that Spurger had poured. "Two shots and another poured."

"Bankers hours," Spurger said. "Are you always on duty?"

"Me or Jude," Frank said.

"We must not have made ourselves clear when we hired you and Jude," Spurger said. "We—the City Council and other community leaders—want you boys to confine your duties to the niggers and the riff-raff."

Frank took a sip of lemonade. He was as calm as an oyster in a shell.

"We don't allow our kind to be arrested. We take care of our own," Spurger said. He handed Frank a slip of paper. "We've put together a list of citizens we don't want arrested. If they give you trouble, just let me know and we'll take care of the problem."

Frank took the paper and carefully read the names. It was a long list. He looked at me and gave Spurger a beatific smile. "I certainly appreciate your clarifying this issue Robert," he said. "Thank you for this list. I will certainly keep an eye out for these outstanding citizens."

Frank stood and shook hands with Spurger.

I stood and nodded toward Spurger's enforcers at the bar. Spurger turned and left the saloon, followed by Stardust and the two hooligans.

"Wise as an owl," Frank said.

Chapter 20

FROM THE JAILHOUSE porch, Frank and I watched the sun disappear behind the distant trees, leaving a pinkish glow in the western sky. A man in a business suit wearing a derby hat scurried down the boardwalk, late for supper probably.

In the fading light, the Blackwell gang rode into town. Outside the Throop Saloon, they stopped and read the city rules Frank and I had posted. They smirked and walked into the Throop Saloon carrying.

Frank knew that I had fought against them in the Taylor County War when I was sheriff of Buffalo Gap. The gang consisted of four hired guns—Berle Blackwell, Willy Willard, Carl Morris, and Hilton Hutton. When together, all four of these bitter contemptuous men reminded me of a hungry wolf pack who killed without remorse. Each one could stomp on their grandma's face and laugh all the way to the saloon. Berle Blackwell always had Colts in low hanging holsters strapped to both legs. When you see somebody wearing two guns, you think lollypops and sodas. Not Blackwell. He was rattlesnake deadly. Shotgun skilled bartenders didn't challenge him when he failed to pay for drinks.

Willy Willard wreaked havoc, fighting and shooting up bars when he was drunk. The alcohol shakes made him unreliable with a gun. Except of the pigpen smell, he was harmless when he slept. The rest of the time he was drunk.

Hilton Hutton was as big as an ox and twice as dumb. He always did what Berle said. He once sucker punched a farmer just because Berle told him to. He ripped out three bars at the Dumas jail but still couldn't get out on the account of his size.

I told Frank that the only guy that really bothered me was Carl Morris. That dirty little runt bragged all around the Estacado that he was going to kill me. "You can count on braggers being cowards and cowards being back shooters," I said.

Frank got up walked to the porch rail and spat into the street. "A back shooter makes you look for excuses to kill him right quick," he said.

I went inside the office to get my takedown. We sauntered over to the Throop Saloon. On our way, John Paul Keelan, who owned the cotton mill stopped us. "Don't go in there, boys. It will be five desperadoes verses two. You wouldn't stand a chance."

This miffed Frank and me too.

By the time we got to the Throop Saloon, Ballard had drunk enough to cause him to stagger against the bar. When I asked for his gun, Ballard lurched toward me. I hit him with my Dragoon. He thudded to the floor.

"Sometimes too many drinks is not enough," Frank said.

When Hudson saw Ballard fall, he rushed toward us with his arms outstretched as if he were going to wrap his arms around us and crush us against each other. Hudson towered above us. Gargantuan inadequately describes his size. Brobdingnagian fits better. Hudson was colossal, but slow. We both stepped aside. Hudson kept moving forward. Like a huge ship, he took a long time to turn around. When he did, Frank kicked him in the groin, causing Hudson to double in pain, exposing his jaw to Frank's upward kick. A sickening sound echoed through the room when Hudson's mandible shattered.

I saw the dirty, little coward Morris sneaking out a side door. He stopped when I yelled. I put my shotgun on the bar. He cowered against the wall. I walked over and slapped him on the face.

A woman gasped.

"Draw," I said. I slapped him again, making a sound like a bullwhip lashing against flesh. "Draw, you coward," I said. "I'm unarmed ... fire away, you coward ... you bragged all over the staked plains that you would kill me. Here I am; shoot me."

The crowd seemed mesmerized. Morris looked toward Frank who was standing nonchalantly leaning against the bar.

I slapped again. Morris flinched. All eyes were upon him. Morris slumped down as if he were about to cry. He took in a deep breath and drew his gun. He pointed it toward me. Frank pulled his gun and shot Morris full in the chest. Morris propelled backward against the wall, a look of surprise on his face. Blood oozed from his mouth. He slumped to the floor, dead.

The people in the saloon looked amazed, impressed. Three men down in a matter of minutes. They looked toward us stupefied.

"Wilson and a renegade with two guns left just before you got here. They said they were heading for the P.A. Smith Hotel," the bartender said.

Frank and I walked toward the Smith Hotel. The disappearing sun cast a golden glow over the town. The townspeople sensed danger. Those on the street moved to the sidewalks. Most of the bystanders scurried inside.

Suddenly, a wisp of a man rushed toward us. "Wilson and a man wearing two guns are outside the hotel, waiting for you. They look tough, sure of themselves. They say they are going to gun you down."

We nodded, and walked on. "Steady and fast," I said.

"Those that have their emotions under control almost always win," Frank said.

"Grace under pressure."

We found Stanley and Whip Wilson outside the Smith Hotel. They smirked at us. Had they been drinking? Otherwise, how could they be so cocky? I pumped my shotgun. Ka-chung. They seemed unimpressed. I held it down by my side. We got about 12-feet from them.

Frank called out, "Put your hands up boys. We came for your firearms."

Wilson drew. He fired at Frank. Missed. Simultaneously, Frank fired three shots in rapid succession. Bam! Bam! Bam! His first shot hit Wilson in the right shoulder. His second shot tore through Wilson's neck. His third shot hit Wilson dead-center in the chest. At the same, time Stanley went for his gun. I raised my shotgun to hip level. The blast almost cut him in half.

People rushed off the streets and out of buildings. Most of the crowd clustered around the bodies, gaping at the wounds and the blood. Some crowded around Frank and me with wonder in their eyes. A boy, probably around 10-years-old, stared up at Frank and me.

"You must be the fastest gunmen in the whole world," he said.

We were the fastest today, but you never know," Frank said. "I wouldn't recommend getting in our line of work."

We turned and walked toward the jailhouse. The crowd parted for us. The boy followed. "Can I have one of your bullets?" he asked Frank.

"Can't spare 'em. Besides supper will satisfy you more. Go home to your mama."

When we reached the jailhouse, Frank said, "Not much in the way of reinforcements."

Chapter 21

THAT NIGHT, WE HEARD that a man had loaded up on whiskey and shot up the Chrystal Ball saloon. When we got there, the drunk was dancing on the top of the bar and singing, "Take Me Out to the Ball Game." Frank grabbed the man's right leg and jerked. The drunk tumbled off the bar and landed on the floor. The fall knocked the man's wind out of him. He lay there gasping for air.

"I'm Marshal Frank Hamer. What's your name?" Frank asked.

Gulping air, the man wheezed, "Robert B. Cameron, Publisher of *The Clansman: A Historical Romance of the Ku Klux Klan* by Thomas Dixon, Jr."

"You seem like an important man," Frank said. "Let me see if you are on my list."

Frank pulled Spurger's note out of his pocket and began reading down the list. "Yes, indeed. Isn't that special? I see that you are on the do not arrest list. Being beholden to the community leaders, I will not arrest you."

Cameron relaxed and smiled at the crowd.

"I will incarcerate you instead," Frank said with a crooked smile. "But first, I want you to give me your gun."

"I don't have a gun," Robert B. Cameron replied.

Frank gave Cameron a ghastly kick in the ribs. "My foot says you do, and when my foot gets a confirmation, it keeps kicking until the gun is found."

"Here's his gun," a skimpily dressed barmaid said, pulling a small 4-barrell pepperbox pistol out of her deep cleavage. "He surrendered it to me for a kiss and a promise."

Frank took the gun and looked down at Cameron who was holding his ribs and moaning. "Now on your feet and git to the jail. I'll be there directly to lock you up."

Cameron stumbled to his feet and walked shakily out of the saloon and headed for the jail.

"Mayor Spurger gave me a no arrest list," Frank said to the saloon crowd. "I thought it was mighty neighborly of him to share suggestions made by the community leaders. There were some mighty prominent people on that list. After researching the list, I decided it gave improper advantage to the prominent. Under my law as Marshal of Navasota, all people are equal. The poorest of the poor, the blackest of the black will be treated as fairly as Mayor Spurger and his so-called community leaders. Anyone and everyone who fails to follow the city rules that you will find posted all over town will be arrested and jailed until bail or a trial date is set."

As Frank was talking, I surveyed the crowd. The opinions were just about split in half. The poorly dressed sided with Frank; the barkeeper, wait staff and other employees seemed to like what Frank said. We had made enemies out of the others. Frank stood as I had seen him many times before, his right hand dangling below his gun holster, his left hand on his hip. He steely and steadily looked everyone in the eye one by one. The he gave that cocked smile, turned, and walked away.

We caught up with Cameron staggering toward the jailhouse a half-block before he reached the front door. A tall woman came running up the street. She wore a tweed, pleated jacket, and a long skirt. Unburdened by a corset, she moved like an athlete. She had a whimsical look, accentuated by emerald-green eyes. Her auburn hair coiled in a bun on the top of her head. When she reached us, she gave Frank an expectant look like a woman who usually gets her way.

"Marshal Hamer, I'm Mollie Cameron," she said extending her hand.

Frank took it, tipped his hat toward her, and pointed in my direction. "The big man is my deputy, Jude McAbee," he said.

"I know. Bigger than you even. The big man who always carries a shotgun," she said, giving me a convivial smile. She had a mystical, beguiling way about her. Made me want to cuddle.

"And I've heard about you," she said smiling winsomely at Frank. "They say you are a humble, God-fearing man who believes in law and order. I do too. I am a Methodist, a practical Methodist, a forgiving Methodist. I believe rules have exceptions."

Frank grinned at her. "I'm a Baptist. I believe in Judgment Day," he said bantering with her. He seemed to enjoy her pluck. I, too, have a weakness for pretty, spirited women. An attractive woman with an enticing smile can win men over right quick.

"My brother is a noble, hardworking man who hardly ever drinks and goes to First Methodist with me every Sunday. Today, he heard the numbers on the book he has published. *The Clansman* is sold out in Houston, Dallas, and Austin and is even doing well in the Texas panhandle where there are no Negro problems."

"That's because they hang any Negro who stays in town after sundown," Frank said with disgust.

"That's not the point," Mollie said. "The point is that my brother was celebrating the good news and got carried away. Being a reasonable man, you can understand that a Methodist who drinks much less than a Baptist away from home can find himself unexpectedly inebriated with a thimbleful of liquor."

Frank listened expectantly, trying to suppress a smile. I couldn't help it. I grinned like a schoolboy skipping school. I liked Mollie's turn of phrase. I wondered where she had attended finishing school. Robert had slumped to the street and was peacefully snoring.

"So, Marshal, I know you are a sensible man who can see that my brother will do no further harm," she said. "He will rest better in his soft bed at home than in your rock-hard tiny cot in a jail cell. Tomorrow morning, he will be up and at it. He has a train ticket to New York that leaves at nine o'clock tomorrow. He has an appointment with an important man, David W. Griffith."

"Griffith? Never heard of him. I don't hear much of anything in the Trans-Pecos except the splashing, sloshing, swimming sound wetbacks make crossing the Rio Grande," Frank said.

"If you haven't heard of D. W. Griffith, you will soon," Mollie said. "He is an entertainment innovator. He has this camera that makes pictures while people are moving. They call it moving pictures. He has made over 40 of these moving pictures this year. He has people act out a drama. These dramas last maybe five minutes or so. The camera takes pictures but can't record sounds. The actors can't be heard in the pictures. They just exaggerate their movements. They make contorted faces at each other—push and shove, that sort of thing."

"You can find that kind of behavior in any Texas saloon," Frank said, grinning. "Does your brother want to be an actor in these moving picture dramas? If so, the way he looks now, he wouldn't be a good candidate."

"No. He wants to talk to Mr. Griffith about making the book he's published—*The Clansman*, into a moving picture drama. Robert wants him to call it *The Birth of a Nation*, referring to the Ku Klux Klan nation, of course.

Frank folded his arms over his chest, smoldering. I was indignant. Mollie noticed.

"I don't approve of the Klan idea myself, but he's my brother," she said with a saucy expression.

"The Klan is made up of a bunch of nameless cowards," Frank said with a gritty expression. "I agree one hundred percent," Mollie said with sincerity in her voice. "Anyone who can immobilize the Klan is my hero."

Frank shrugged and put his hands in his pockets in a aw-shucks-I'm-your-man sort of way. There was a pause in the conversation. Mollie seemed more interested in Frank than her brother.

"Anyway," Mollie said coming out of her reverie, Robert needs his rest so he can do his best job. He will sleep much better at home than in a jail cell. We all do better when we rest well."

Frank and I stood there. We didn't say anything.

"Your healthy and vibrant looks tell me you take good care of yourself, and that you rest well," Mollie said looking at Frank. "You wouldn't want to deprive another successful man from his well-needed rest, sleeping in his own comfortable bed."

I thought that if Mr. Cameron could sleep comfortably in a dusty street, he could sleep anywhere with no difficulty tonight.

Frank took off his hat and held it over his heart. He spoke with deference and with the politeness of a Texas gentleman. "Well 'ma'am," he said. "You certainly are a smooth debater who I would want on my side in any contest. I respect your temerity. You make some awful good points, but if I make an exception to the city rules, my authority will be lost. People will think I'm a weak-livered hypocrite who kowtows to pretty women with gumption. I'm a Baptist for sure, but I'm not a hypocrite."

"And I'm a Methodist—and like I said, a practical one. Would a good Baptist take some money to put in the collection plate in exchange for releasing my brother?" Molly asked nonchalantly as if she already knew the answer.

Frank put his Stetson back on his head and tipped it toward Molly. "Instead, why not contribute to the Methodist Home—the orphanage in Waco," Frank said airily. "In the meantime, I will carry Mr. Cameron to his tiny cot in a cozy jail cell. I will be at the jailhouse early in the morning. You can post bail then and get Mr. Cameron on the train to Houston."

With that, Frank picked up Mr. Cameron like he was a bag of potatoes, threw him over his shoulder, and ambled toward the jail. When I looked back, Mollie was standing with her hands on her hips, smiling.

Chapter 22

MOLLIE ENTERED THE jailhouse door just as the sun cast an orange glow over the town. She wore a full-length body-clinging dress that accentuated her hourglass figure. The puffed high collar and wide brimmed hat with an ostrich feather gave her an aristocratic look. The blended rouge on her cheeks complemented her creamy complexion. She looked terrific. Frank noticed. He took the bail money she offered with a gentlemanly nod. I fetched our drunk.

Mr. Cameron, slimmer and taller than he appeared last night, held his head down shamefully. He looked like every other hung-over man I had seen before: terrible. Bird nest hair, blood shot eyes, droopy lids, stubble over a sickly pale face that was wrinkled on one side from lying in one place too long. He walked with an unsteady carefulness. His hands trembled. His breath smelled worse than a rotting hog that had been dead for three days. I wondered if he would clean up quickly enough to make the nine o'clock train to New York.

"Sheriff Hamer, I know you're pleased with yourself. You can mark that down in your log book: another drunk jailed," Mollie said with a plucky look.

"Yes, ma'am, when someone pulls a gun and starts shootin' up a place, we generally jail 'em," Frank said.

"Or shoot them," Mollie said with a teasing tone.

"That has happened from time to time."

"You like killing men?"

"When it's him or me, I have little choice," Frank said.

"But when you have a drunk whose sister wants to take him home ... you do have a choice. And you chose the arrogant way just to show a woman you could. I say that a man who has to prove he is a man is a weak man," Mollie said with a coquettish smile.

"Whoa!" Frank said with a boyish grin. "You are too fast for me. You twist things around so that my mind can't tell my tongue what to say. First you suggest I'm a killer, and then you call me a weak man. I say you have a killer tongue that my weak tongue cannot match."

"A man that hath a tongue, I say is no man if with his tongue he cannot win a woman," Mollie said.

"Sounds like Shakespeare to me. How about this, Miss Finishing School showoff? You're as tantalizing as a dream. I'd like to ride past yonder with you."

"Let's hallelujah the county," Mollie countered.

These two were faster with words than double-struck lightening. If I hadn't been there, I would have said somebody must have written that down on paper. But I was there, and that is exactly how it happened. Yes, they were in love and fast out of the shoot to tell each other about it.

Mr. Cameron, who had been sitting in a stupor, sat up and looked around as if he just realized he was in a jailhouse. He suddenly remembered what had happened the night before. He apologized for his behavior and gave Mollie a deferential look. She shrugged, kissed him on the cheek, put her arm around him, and led him out the door.

"She loves him," I said.

"He's her brother," Frank said with that boyish grin.

"I wonder what he looks like when he's shaved and bathed. Family genetics you know. He's tall. He could be as handsome as she is pretty," I said.

"That would take a spectacular cleanup job," Frank said.

"Tall, handsome men have an advantage that short men never realize," I said.

"Unless they're dumb. There's nothing more pathetic than a tall, handsome, dumb man," Frank said.

"What about a tall, handsome, dumb and broke man?" I asked.

"Handsome or ugly; tall or short; rich or poor, we've all got to play the hand we've been dealt," Frank said. "I think Mollie might be my winning hand."

Chapter 23

JIMMY LEE'S BECAME our choice for relaxing. After we made our late afternoon rounds—walking or riding the Navasota streets just to let everyone know that we were present and watching—we ambled over to Jimmy Lee's saloon. Just before evening, I was sitting at our favorite corner table reading *The Virginian* by Owen Wister. From time to time, I would look out on the street and watch the setting sun color the town with a warm golden glow. Frank threw the owls a few peanuts and began improving Sir Newton's vocabulary.

"Pistol" he said, pulling his Colt out of the holster and pointing to it.

"Pistol," Sir Newton said.

"Pistol," Frank said, again pointing to his gun.

"Pistol," the macaw said.

Frank replaced the Colt in the holster and pulled it out again. He pointed to the Colt and shrugged toward Sir Newton.

"Pistol," Sir Newton answered.

Frank walked over with a glass of lemonade in his hand. I was sipping on Jack Daniel's. Old #7 is hard to beat. "Sir Newton is smarter than all the Mexicans west of the Trans Pecos," he said.

"It's fairly easy for Sir Newton to learn concrete words like pistol, bullet, and whiskey, but what about words like happy and sad?"

"I wouldn't burn any daylight teaching him that," Frank said. "All I'd

97

have to do would be to make a face to indicate the meaning of those two words, and he would learn them as quickly as he learned pistol."

"All right, then," I said. "What about love? Even more difficult—can you teach him what romance means?"

Frank shrugged his shoulders and grinned. "I'll teach him some Shakespeare sonnets instead."

As swiftly as a peregrine falcon zooms for its quarry, Frank became serious. Shakespeare sonnets can have that effect. Frank ordered a whiskey from Jimmy who poured him a shot.

In past conversations, Frank had told me that he never felt easy around women. Most of the Pecos River women were rough and tough, almost masculine, pioneer women. He became uncomfortable when reading about the craze for newness and innovation that seemed to possess big city Texas women. He had a vague feeling that these women were silly and shallow, delicate, and needy. He admitted to using women for sexual pleasure but never considered love with the requirements of a settled lifestyle to be in the cards.

The warm glow of this evening and a few sips of whiskey seemed to loosen Frank's tongue. "All of those ideas I had about women changed when I met Mollie," he said. "That first night, her intelligence and her brassy personality attracted me. I had never been around such a spirited woman. I didn't sleep well that night thinking about her," he said.

Frank had never talked about women that way. I stirred in my chair and leaned forward a little, listening.

"The next day her warm tenderness made me want to reach out and hold her in my arms. Those emerald green eyes, her complexion, and auburn hair swept me away."

Men don't talk to other men like that, I thought. *It must be the whiskey.* I didn't tell Frank I felt the same way. I, too, had fallen in love with her. What self-confident man wouldn't fall for a bright and spirited woman with undeniable charm? A self-reliant woman frightens timid men—but galvanizes the confident ones. Scintillating women enrapture self-confident men.

From the way Frank and Mollie interacted that first night, I knew they had a special attraction for each other that excluded me. I would love her, but I would never have her. I had a melancholy feeling I would never find a woman that could fill my heart the way Mollie did.

When we are in love, most of us can't stop talking about the loved one. Frank certainly couldn't. When Frank and I were together, he told me almost everything about Mollie. Mollie's mother died in childbirth, and Mollie grew up with her older brother on her father's vast ranch. She rode the range, rounded up the cattle, roped 'em, branded 'em, and doctored 'em with her father by her side. She adored him with his tough yet tender ways and became deeply disappointed in herself when she failed to please him. When her father died from a stroke, she retreated to her room for six weeks.

Frank told me she excelled in rodeo barrel racing and calf roping but couldn't boil water and refused any household chores. Their colored maid Emma did the cooking, washing, and cleaning. Emma lived in a tiny cottage with Ernesto, her common law husband, across the winding tree-lined road leading to the big ranch house. Ernesto served as a do-it-all handyman. Mollie spent time riding over the family's vast estate. At other times, she practiced rope tricks or hunted. When her tomboy days inevitably ended, she became a Smith College woman, her alma mater—a woman few could match in grace and gentility.

When I saw Mollie and Frank holding hands, or when their eyes were focused on each other, or when they talked with cheerful animation, my heart ached with a disconsolate joy. I both delighted in their love for each other and was haunted by unrequited love. I loved Mollie too. My heart swelled when she was around.

I wondered if I would find Stardust as enchanting as Mollie. The notes from Stardust warmed my heart. When we had time together, would Stardust love me as deeply as Mollie loved Frank? Would I love her more than I love Mollie?

Chapter 24

SOME OF THE TOWNSPEOPLE began to see that Frank had a deep conviction of impartiality, evenhandedness, fair-mindedness; he believed in justice and counted on the courts to exact justice without prejudice. His father and later Captain Rogers had instilled in him a duty to protect the weak from the strong. When unprovoked, he was modest, unassuming, and humble.

Nonetheless, I often became concerned about his temper that was easily aroused. He didn't hesitate to take unpopular positions or defend unpopular causes. He was eminently self-confident, aggressive, and afraid of no one, no threat, and no danger, but on rare occasions when someone ignored his commands, insulted him, or called him "a nigger lover" his anger overwhelmed his common sense, and he would lose control. He was especially enraged when the guilty remained unpunished.

We were walking the streets making rounds when we heard a ferocious growling and barking followed by a terrible high-pitched yelp. A powerful pit-bull had attacked an older black woman. Three or four men were standing around, laughing, and urging the dog.

"Sic 'em" one of the men kept saying.

The dog had a death hold on the woman's leg who was screaming and thrashing, trying to get away. Frank pulled out his big .45 and hit the dog on his head knocking him out cold.

The sunlight seemed to focus more intensely over Frank, giving his face a luminescent radiance. His entire body seemed to glow with strength and power. "Leave this woman alone," he said, his voice sounding like wind rushing through the canyons. The men backed up, fear in their eyes; then they turned and fled.

Frank turned toward a few black people gathering around the woman, an aw-shucks smile on his relaxed face, his blue eyes calm and warm.

A colored man said, "Sur' proud that ya done somethin' about that dog, Marshal Frank. He's dunt attacked three black folks, near' killed one 'fore he be pull'd off. Nipped a bunch more passin' on the street. Kilt bunch of nigger's dogs, some of 'em right good dogs, pointers and 'trivers. The white folk theys just stand by, laughin,' holler sick 'em. Mr. Red train 'em to go after us coloreds."

About that time, a red headed, barrel-chested man with broad shoulders and bulging muscles ran out of Texas Red's Saloon. He carried a baseball bat. He started screaming at Frank about hitting his dog.

"That dog is my watch dog. Keeps niggers and ner-do-wells out of my saloon. You can't go hitting on my dog. He's private property."

Frank reached up his powerful hands, his forearms bulging from years pounding the anvil at his father's blacksmith workshop, and with his flat palms open, he whacked the saloonkeeper on both ears. The bear-like blow crumpled the man to the ground, and the baseball bat fell away from his hand.

"The city law we posted doesn't allow dogs to run wild on the streets," Frank said. "If your dog attacks another animal or person without cause, I'll shoot him."

Slowly the man stood, wobbling. Without a word, the bartender nestled the unconscious dog in his arms and staggered back into the saloon.

A few days later, the pit bull again ran loose and after a ferocious fight, killed a blue heeler. When Frank heard about the kill, he strolled into Texas Red's saloon, pulled his Colt, and shot the pit bull dead.

Texas Red screamed, "You can't do that. The Texas Supreme Court ruled that it's unconstitutional to shoot loose animals if they have an owner. You can't kill personal property without due process of law."

"Well I guess the Texas Supreme Court hasn't read my city rules 'cause I just killed your dog," Frank said and walked out the door with Texas Red cussing at him.

Chapter 25

I LAY ALONGSIDE THE woman with the beguiling walk. She had thick raven hair that bathed the contour of her oval face and cascaded over her ample bosom. Her burnished golden-brown skin was as luxuriant as silk. Eyelashes arched over feline Eden-green eyes. Her full lips and wide mouth showed ivory-white teeth when she smiled. She was a beautiful woman unmatched by most, except for Mollie, my heart's desire, and few others, but now, at this time, and in this place, nothing could compare with the splendor of her warmth.

She had a radiant personality despite, or perhaps as a defense against, inconstant circumstances. She had Mexican and Comanche blood. Lieutenant Randy Moung captured her after a failed Comanche raid at Questa. After he killed two soldiers who tried to steal her, he fled the army, working odd jobs throughout the Southwest to support his gambling habits. He lost her when a gambler's straight flush beat his ace-high full house. The gambler taught her seductive ways to distract the other card players as he hornswoggled them. In Dallas, Spurger, more interested in winning at poker than ogling enticing women, shot the gambler dead for cheating. She then became Spurger's slave and mistress.

Spurger lied about leading a reform group to the Dallas eastside. There was no reform group. There was no Frolic Club. Spurger went to Dallas to gamble. He returned to Navasota with a pocketful of money—and a handful of a woman. She scratched him. Clawed him. Bit him. Spit on him. Each time, he locked her in her room for one week without food. Eventually she stopped resisting him, but her spirit remained undaunted. She hated him with the ferocity of a lion in her heart.

We become infatuated with people in various ways: the way a person talks ... or walks, a smile across a crowded room, the tinkling tremble of a distant laugh, a touch of the hand, a shimmering glance. That first day in the courthouse conference room her gaze captured me.

On an overcast autumn day, Spurger had taken the train to attend the Annual Texas Bankers Convention in Dallas, leaving Stardust at his mansion. Early in the evening, Stardust startled me when she suddenly appeared from behind an oak and reached for my hand as I walked to my cabin in the woods. I clasped her hand and led her through the cabin door. My spare one-room cabin had two windows in the front and the back, a bed, and a small chair left of the door opposite a wood stove, and a hutch on the right. There was a small table and two deer-hide seated chairs in the middle of the room. No decorations festooned the stark one-room cabin.

A lightning flash followed by rolling thunder broke my reverie. It began to rain, softly at first, and then the drizzle increased into a torrential downpour. Here we were alone together for the first time in a cabin nestled in the woods, stirred by the rhythm of the rain on the roof, the cloudburst throwing a curtain over the outside world. We felt safely cocooned against interruption—insulated against intrusion.

Stardust dropped her hand from mine and turned toward me. I put my arms around her. I smelled the faint freshness of evergreen. She ran her hands up my back. She reached up to embrace my neck. I wrapped my arms around her and held her close. Her breasts crushed against my chest; I lowered my head, and we kissed. Her moist lips were like gardenias bathed in morning due.

Later as we lay together, her head cradled on my shoulder, I gazed into nothingness blissfully bewildered. I had encountered the indescribable sensation of loving and being loved.

Thoughts of women I had been with before flashed through my mind. Barmaids. An Indian or two. A schoolmistress. A widow. The lonely and the desperate. In those past times when evening waned, I was gone with no regards, no regrets. I'd had a few lingering relationships, but eventually, I'd go just as they thought I would. As I embraced Stardust in my arms, I wondered if leaving had been left behind.

Then I thought of Mollie ... how much I loved her. Can I love two people with burning intensity? I'd never held Mollie in my arms, but my love for her burned in my heart ... but I would never have her return my love. And Frank—I loved him as a brother. I could never betray him.

I love Jesus too, but I'm not living a life worthy of Him. My dalliances with women would not please him. Did I love Jesus as much as I love Mollie? Did I love Jesus as much as I love Stardust? They are 'beautiful, and therefore to be wooed.'

"You are a woman and therefore to be won," I whispered to myself.

I am a graduate from Yale Divinity School and a former Methodist circuit rider. Now I'm a gunslinger, a killer, an adulterer, and a conflicted and confused man ... I thought of the verse from Paul's letter to the Romans: O *wretched man that I am who shall deliver me from the body of this death?* These thoughts whirled in my mind....

My musings returned to pressing issues when Stardust opened her eyes and stirred.

"What about Spurger?" I asked.

"After fifteen years with the Comanche, do you not think I learned their ways?"

Chapter 26

WE WERE IN THE OFFICE. Frank groaned and moaned about paperwork; with his head bowed, a pencil in his hand, a well-used eraser nearby, he looked more like a disgruntled boy made to stay after school than a Texas Ranger.

I was contemplating Shakespeare's Sonnet 30 when two men burst into the office. Both were wearing bib overalls, straw hats, and waders. I later learned the fishermen's names: twins, Jasper and Casper Burham. I also learned that these two took a long time to get to the point. Their frenetic excitement caused their voices to raise a pitch higher than normal, but they told their detailed story from beginning to end.

"I was enjoying our moonshine whiskey in a jug—it was a wondrous hot day, and sweat was pouring off me," Casper said. "Besides I've found that the fish bite better when I'm a little tipsy. I took a big ole chugalug when Jasper yelled that he found something."

"I was standing about a foot deep in the Navasota," Jasper said. "I felt a tug on my line. I jerked the line with no results. I tugged some more, but nothing moved. 'The line is caught on something,' I said to myself. I was disgusted. I waded out into the river, following the caught line. I was tugging hard on the line as I walked. The water got deep. It was up to my chin when I tugged again, and a body popped up. I yelled to Casper, 'Hey we got a body here.'"

"I waded out to help Jasper pull the body ashore," Casper said. "We turned the body over and saw that it was a woman—a right pretty one. Her throat had been cut from ear to ear. She couldn't have been in the river long because nothing was shrived and dried up, nor bloated neither. The 'gators, and catfish hadn't gotten to her."

"We jumped in the wagon and drove up here faster than Cooter Brown gets drunk, and here we are to tell you that there's a body in our wagon," Jasper said.

My heart sank when Casper mentioned the victim was a pretty woman. Frank and I rushed outside and peered into the wagon. Frank pulled a ragged blanket back.

"Stardust," I said as my knees collapsed. I folded onto the ground.

"Hardy's knife work," Frank said.

"Spurger's instructions."

"Need proof," Frank said.

Stardust's murder engulfed me. What? How? Where? When? Why? Within minutes, anger overwhelmed my grief. No. Anger was not a strong enough word. *Rage* better explained my reaction to Stardust's murder. My rage kindled vengeance! I could not leave vengeance to the Lord. I must seek retribution!

I knew who did it—Pack with his long knife; I knew who ordered it—Spurger with his quest for dominance. I would kill them. I didn't care how long I would have to wait, if I could only do it at last. I hoped they would not die before I killed them.

Spurger must have known of the bond Stardust and I shared. How? Did the cook tell him? What about Mildred? Did she reveal our secret? Had someone else seen us in the few minutes we had alone? Had he noticed the glances we shared?

All these suspicions, thoughts, ideas, and feelings raced through my mind as I collapsed into a chair crying. I pulled myself together quickly. Frank let me talk. He poured me a glass of whiskey. I rambled. After a long while, he left to fetch Mollie.

I calmed somewhat. I began to think twice about vengeance. If I murdered Spurger and Hardy, would I be any better than they? Vengeance would certainly lead to my destruction.

Perhaps my Yale education was valuable after all, for I thought of Shakespeare's *Hamlet*. Hamlet's anger toward his uncle for murdering his father caused his need for vengeance. His anger was understandable, just like my anger, but his quest for vengeance caused him to accidently kill Polonius. After Polonius died, he continued to seek vengeance, leading to the death of his betrothed Olivia, his mother, his brother, and his uncle; eventually, Hamlet died from a poisoned sword.

Hmm ... I thought about this: *is vengeance poison?* Perhaps. *Yes, vengeance poisons the soul.*

My mind raced. As I contemplated Hamlet's dilemma, I thought of Heathcliff of *Wuthering Heights*, who stopped at nothing to get vengeance. His revenge plot eventually left him with nothing but madness and destructive consequences. He died alone and unhappy.

In the *Divine Comedy* by Dante, those repenting of anger in purgatory are blinded by smoke. Vengeance perhaps blinds us to reality. We don't think straight.

All these thoughts raced through my mind when Frank and Mollie returned. My thinking was clouded with grief, anger, and perhaps a little too much whiskey. I couldn't hear or understand all that they said. Frank said something about losing control when he became angry. Mollie agreed that Frank's anger concerned her, also. They discussed this for a while.

And then I clearly heard Mollie say, "Grief often wraps your entire being with anger."

A little later, I heard Frank say, "Righteous anger rises up when someone sins against God's law."

"Yes, but that does not give us permission for retribution. 'Vengeance is mine sayeth the Lord.'"

"That's a tough command," Frank said.

"Life is difficult," Mollie said.

It could not have been long after when I feel asleep, for I was weary with grief and anger. I soon began to dream. In my dream, I saw an enraged alligator snarling and snapping as the air stirred the muddy waters. Twisting and turning, he bit himself repeatedly. Then he choked on the splashing water churned by his frenetic leaping. Next, I saw a water moccasin stuck in mud, hissing loudly with a deep and steady warning of sullen wrath. Then lying in wait for something to strike, he strangled on the muck and mire of the swampy water. I partially awoke drowsy, but frightened. Almost immediately, I fell into a deep slumber.

Chapter 27

STARDUST'S FUNERAL DID nothing to relieve my rage. Spurger, wifeless and childless, sat in the front pew with Hardy. A mistress who resides in secret has few friends. Nonetheless, Spurger's associates and those indebted to him, and those who feared him, filled the sanctuary. Those whose wealth flourished through bank loans occupied the front church pews as they contemplated future loans. Merchants, cowhands from his ranch, bank officers, aids, assistants, and other employees filled the next few rows. Acquaintances, neighbors, and church members compelled by tradition sat in the next few pews. Frank, Mollie, and I sat in the corner of the last pew.

The funeral message came directly from the Baptist Church Manuel. There were no eulogies. Then Spurger got up and walked to the pulpit slowly and hesitatingly, as if he suffered from a deep and profound grief. Wiping his eyes that were dryer than the West Texas desert, he mumbled a few inaudible words.

After pulling out a handkerchief to blow his nose, he cleared his throat and said, "All of you know that Stardust served my home for several years. She cooked meals, washed dishes, swept the floors, made the beds—all the things that maids do. Occasionally, she would come to town with me to shop for groceries and such. Sometimes she would serve the aldermen at our meetings. She was a kind and gentle soul who had a difficult life ...

indeed, when I found her on a missionary trip to Dallas, she was swamped in squalor and sin. I am pleased that through my Christian witness she gave her life to Christ right here in this church."

Spurger wiped his eyes again. He seemed to totter and almost fall. With a dramatic act, he gained his composure and cleared his throat again.

In a stentorian and harsh voice, he thundered, "And now the dear departed maid whom I loved as a sweet sister has been murdered most viciously. I believe a man killed my Christian maid out of jealous rage. This malicious spiteful man must be punished. Anyone who has proof against this man will receive a $5,000 reward."

Then, holding a handkerchief to his face, Spurger stumbled to his seat where he received condolences from a line of well-wishers. Frank had to unobtrusively restrain me. When I had calmed somewhat, the three of us decided to have a drink at Jimmy Lee's saloon.

As we sat at the back table, I raged and fumed while drowning my grief in whiskey. The saloon did a booming business after the funeral. Talk turned to other things: the Barnum and Bailey Circus that was coming to town; the Presidential race between Republican William Howard Taft and Democrat William Jennings Bryan; the expected launch next year of the Model T Ford priced at $850. A few men argued about the best pitcher in Major League Baseball, Christy Mathewson or Leonard Johnson; others discussed Coach Ned Merriam of the fightin' Texas Aggies and their upcoming game with the tea sippers at the University of Texas; and as always weather, ranching, and farming entered the conversations. By and by we left.

The next morning, I recalled another dream: I saw a boxing ring made extra small to insure constant battle. In the ring, two tank-like bruisers pounded each other with piteous ferocity. One fighter with blackened eyes and ears thickened into cauliflowers had *Murder* tattooed on his chest. He fought in a plodding, machine-like style, grinding away at his opponent whose nose and mouth dripped copiously with blood that poured down his scar-riddled face. On his chest, the word *Vengeance* stood out in scarred letters. Ringside, horrible monsters in spiked chairs clamored for more blood. An impish figure—a short, round, balding man with a broad gnomic face and wearing a blooded referee uniform pointed down a long hallway. As far as the eye could see, cramped boxing rings crowded the hall. Each ring had bleeding fighters pounding away at each other.

Gradually my rage declined to a seething anger. I became increasing frustrated when I understood that vengeance would bring unwelcome repercussions that would ruin my life. When I realized there existed no way to resolve my anger, I became increasingly more despondent. Irresolutely, step-by-step, my grief slowly melted to an unresolved anger locked away deep within my heart.

No one had come forth with information regarding Stardust's killer. I had frequent talks with Mildred who hated Spurger almost as much as I abhorred him. The murder and the aftermath must have taken place in the deepest, darkest part of night just before dawn. Mildred knew of no one who had seen Hardy slash Stardust's throat. Neither had anyone seen her body being dumped into the river. Nevertheless, I had no doubt that Spurger and Hardy had murdered Stardust. My smoldering anger could not be quenched until I saw them both dangling from a rope.

Chapter 28

MOLLIE AND FRANK BEGAN spending more time together, so I recruited Mance to accompany me as I inspected farms and plantations to mitigate the atrocities suffered by the Negro workers. One day I asked Mance to drive me in the buggy out to Walter Mobley's plantation. I had heard Mobley treated the help kindly. I had experienced enough evil. I craved kindness and goodness. I hoped to be encouraged by a visit to Mobley's plantation. On our way to the plantation, Mance did most of the talking:

"My daddy, he give me the name of Emancipation says cause I'm free. I shortened it to Mance cause I ain't free. Ya work on one of them big plantations, ya work from can't to can't. They pay you sure, but it's with tokens to buy groceries and such from their store. If you want to run away and find a better place, the boss man he sends the hounds and a bunch of men after ya and they brang ya back."

Mance hopped out of the buggy to open a gate. "Sounds like you're still a slave," I said.

Mance got back in the buggy, and we started up the plantation road to Walter Mobley's antebellum home. "In one way I ain't free, none of us niggas are free, but I am free in my hawt. I got Jesus Christ in my hawt; I got a joyful hawt. And God give me the talent to share my joy on Satiddy nights when I gets to play my music. Music makes our hawt free. On the plantation when we sang, we free. Sanging stops worries. Sanging makes the time go faster."

As we topped a small rise, we saw an opulent, symmetrical two-story home with four Greek-type columns, evenly spaced windows, elaborate balconies, and covered porches.

Mobley was at the front gate when we arrived. He was a tall, fastidiously dressed man who brushed his silver hair fully away from his unlined forehead. He radiated the cultivated manner and authoritative ease of an eighteenth-century southern gentleman.

Mobley flashed extremely white teeth when he recognized me. He nodded toward Mance with a quizzical look.

"This is Mance Lipscomb," I said. "Frank hired him to help us get around."

"So this is Mance," Mobley said emitting a deep chuckle. "I've heard some of my hired help talk about his guitar playing at their Saturday night suppers. Quite a songster as they say."

Mobley paused and cleared his throat before continuing.

"I'm surprised to see you out here, deputy. You must know I have a good reputation for taking care of my people. It is neither logical nor Christian to mistreat the help. If I take care of them, they will take better care of me. You reap what you sow."

I nodded respectfully as I got down from the buggy. Mance sat ramrod straight in the wagon seat smiling broadly.

"Let me show you around," Mobley said with a slight deferential bow and flourish of his hat pointing behind his home. "I pay my people with American dollars, not tokens. They shop in town because I don't have a company store, and anytime they want to seek better conditions, I support their decision. Of course, like any good businessman, I refuse to tolerate any slackers, miscreants, or trouble makers, but I don't beat them; I dismiss them."

Well behind the house, a washstand and a roofed cistern-supplied shower stood a good distance from two covered picnic tables resting under a stately oak. I could see two-dozen or more blacks working in the fields beyond. North of the home several mules stood in a large corral next to a barn. I looked, but didn't see a bell.

"Very nice place, you have here Mr. Mobley," I said as we returned to the buggy. "Looks like you take good care of the help."

Mr. Mobley shook my offered hand. We walked to the buggy where Mance sat still smiling. "Mance," he said. "I hear that you are more than a superb guitar player. My people say you are a hard worker; you are trustworthy, and loyal. If you want to get back into plantation work sometime, come see me. I can always use a fine young man like you."

"Thank ya sir," Mance said. His smile broadened into a beam of white teeth.

"I imagine you've found that most of the large farms and plantations around here provide excellent conditions for their workers."

I tipped my hat and nodded a smile as we left. *No, I haven't,* I thought. Mobley must be delusional, extremely naïve, or a gentleman, avoiding criticizing others. The working conditions on the other plantations we had visited offered none of the genteel conditions found on the Mobley place. From what Mance had told us, the mistreatment of the blacks stopped for a while after our visits. But within a few weeks, they resumed. The law may be able to impede crime to a certain extent, but the legal system was insufficient to stop the progression of evil. My thoughts cheered when Mance, without losing a beat, began talking again.

"Mista Walter a good man," Mance said. "He do what he say. He's fair man to his hep. That's what they say at the Satidday night suppas. I play up to Sunday mornin when everbody go to church. I can't go to church. The church quit me. Say I hav to stop the gittah playin' or no church. I'm still playin.' God give this talent ta me, what I got, an he satisfied in what I'm doin.' It comes from God this playing and singing power and I don't forget it. I jest say, 'Thank you God for giving this to me.' That's how I can play with joy and to hep people forget their sorrows for a while. An you kin do thangs through God by prayin' an thankin Him."

115

The bright sun made the vast sky sparkle as blue as a baby's eyes. Heat waves rose in the distance. I pulled out my bandana and wiped the sweat off my face.

Mance continued. "Been thankin God for what he done by sendin' you and Mista Frank to hep me. The first thing I pray to God when I knowd I was safe—I thanked God for my fingars and hands. They ain't hurt none and I can keep playing my gittah; worshippin God with my gittah. I want peacefulness and joy in my hawt. An I thank God for you Mista Jude and Mista Frank cause God sent you to brang peace to Navasota."

Mance paused and twisted his body so he could look me square in the face.

"God give you talent to get rid of bad people. It's a gift you got; a gift from God. Just make sure that gift don't wander and you find yourself on the wrong side of the line; that line that separates good from bad. Now that line is awful hard to see most times. That's why you got to look hard. That's why yo gotta pray for Holy Spirit power ever' night. The world is so tangled up you need Holy Spirit protection."

I looked at Mance with wonderment. "Mance," I said, "How did you, at your young age, get to be so wise?"

"God give wisdom to me," he said.

Chapter 29

JUST ABOUT EVERY DAY after I had completed my morning rounds, I would drop by the Emporium for a cup of coffee and a pot full of chatter with Mildred. Usually all her morning customers had finished their breakfasts, leaving the room unoccupied except for the two of us.

Most of the time she filled me with town gossip: whose cow had died; which creek had flooded; how an embezzlement went down; who dyed their hair red; and why the Navasota School Board could find no one to teach French. It seemed that Mildred always provided a spoonful of titillating stories—as she put it 'whose stallion had entered the open barn door,' and such. Generally, her run-away mouth entertained me but gave no useful legal information. From time to time, she would give me some cream and sugar with her chatter that would lead to an arrest or stop a crime. Today was one of those days.

I went to my usual table in the back of the restaurant. From where I sat, I could see the streets and watch for anyone entering the room. As she poured my coffee, Mildred leaned close to my ear. She began talking in a hushed tone. "I've got some news for you," she whispered with a brimful of excitement.

"Well, all right, but I hear better when people talk in a normal tone of voice. I see no eavesdroppers. You can speak up."

"You know Billy-Billy Guidry. He's the redheaded, freckle faced

Cajun," Mildred said loud enough for me to hear, but soft enough to prevent the kitchen help from hearing.

"No. I don't know Billy-Billy Guidry. And there's no such thing as a redheaded, freckle faced Cajun. Cajuns were French-speaking people from Arcadia who came down to Louisiana from Canada in the early 1800s. They have a lilting accent that teases the ears and stimulates a smile."

"Well aren't we being a snot-nosed, Yale College intellectual this morning. Well, Mr. Smarty-pants don't you think an Arcadian can plant his corn in another field? As I was about to say, Billy-Billy Guidry the redheaded, freckle faced Cajun got his name from the fact that his momma was told she was to have twins. She said, 'Lardy, lardy, don't let me have no twin babies. I ain't got time for no two babies at once.'"

Mildred accentuated her gossipy stories by imitating dialects and the way others talked. I'm easily entertained. Just hearing her different accents entertained me.

"So Billy-Billy's mamma, Rosheen, prayed and prayed not to have twins. When Billy came out of the chute all alone, Rosheen happily named her boy Billy-Billy. She said 'I got one for two so 'my chile he 'desurvd ta name a Billy-Billy. The good Lard give me one fer two so he ganna have two names for one. Tat ways I 'member the good Lard blesses his peoples if ye jest pray hard enough.'"

Mildred's engine was unstoppable—full steam ahead. Her facts generally followed a story—a long, long story. Surely she couldn't make this stuff up. Some of it must be true.

"Now Billy-Billy had a father who stuttered real bad. He would say like, 'c-c-c-can you g-g-go to t-t-town w-w-w-with me.' So when he called for Billy-Billy, he would say B-B-Billy; come here B-B-Billy.' Some folks really don't know how Billy-Billy got his name. A few insist his name came by being called Billy-Billy because his father stuttered, but I have it on good authority Billy-Billy got his name on account of his mamma being happy he was one, not two."

Now here Mildred showed her usual style. She would shout down the well listening to her own echoes before hauling-up the water bucket.

"Billy-Billy married this woman Sapphire. Now Sapphire is a light-colored Negro who is hotter than a honeymoon hotel. She swivels every man's neck, if you know what I mean. She oozes sensuality, but she only lets Billy-Billy hoe her cabbage patch. She is not a flirt in any way, but there is something in the way she moves that attracts men like no other woman. She has that warm and tender sexuality that has the tongues of men hanging out like hounds after a rabbit. She doesn't realize she is being pursued. She has no idea what her flawless beauty does to men. No one can catch her. That makes her even more desirable."

I figured that maybe we were about to get to the point, but no—Mildred had more wells to shout down.

"Sapphire's not like these gussied-up women who chase after men. Once caught, the man finds the woman as cold and rigid as a one-day-old corpse. No sir, Sapphire satisfies her man and no other. Go figure. I look at Billy-Billy, and I ask myself how does that happen? He's as plain looking as the Texas panhandle: thin, stringy red hair; a flat nose riddled with freckles; ears that stick out like a flag on a windy day; a gap between his buck teeth; a caved in chest; and spindly legs. Now don't get me wrong Billy-Billy is as nice as he can be. He works as hard as a beaver in a forest. He's as honest as a gold coin. He's as dependable as an ox on Sunday. But I've never heard him say more than two words. When not working, which is most of the time, he sits and whittles. Never makes anything. Just picks up a stick until he's whittled it down to the nub; then he picks up another stick, and goes to whittling again. How could this one in a million woman go for a two-nickel man? Now this is the way I see it. Plain looking men get good looking women because proud men are too vain to ask."'

"Hold it, Mildred. I'm sorry to interrupt. I like hearing your stories, but I've got a meeting with a committee of tenant farmers in a few minutes, so can you get to the point and tell me your secret?"

Mildred looked around the room. "Still nobody here," she said. "The room is as empty as the Easter tomb." She began to whisper. "Sapphire was going into Cashmore's Grocery Store when Spurger pulled her aside. Of course, no one could stop to stare or listen longer than to pass by because his thug Pack Hardy stood near to keep Spurger's conversation private. But here's the juicy part: Spurger put his arm around Sapphire and tried to pull her closer to him so he could whisper something in her ear. Well whatever he said must've been a doozy because that sassy gal reached out and scratched his face, drawing blood! Spurger screamed cursing like a Baptist on vacation. Several people heard him clearly say, 'I will get you for this.' He took out his handkerchief and wiped the blood off his face. He had to wipe several times because the blood just kept on flowing. My sources say he up and turned and slunk away like a whupped dog with his tail between his legs, with his little pup Hardy by his side. But Sapphire stood there with her hands on her hips, arms akimbo, and her legs spread wide, a look of defiance on her face."

I smiled. Mildred's tales never failed to satisfy; notwithstanding the long and winding roads she took getting there. This one was especially rewarding. A woman stood her ground, and Spurger sneaked away. He had his comeuppance at last.

Chapter 30

ON AN AUTUMN DAY brilliant with sunshine, I sat eating vanilla ice cream outside of Kandy's Kitchen. I had just finished breezing through the crossword puzzle in the *Navasota Examiner-Review*. Lou Brickman, a prosperous landowner, came riding up on his horse Thunder whose full-speed gallop made bystanders run for cover and made dogs bark.

When Lou saw me, he pulled on the reins and jumped off Thunder before the stallion came to a complete stop. Breathlessly and quickly, Lou told me that a tenant farmer's wife had been raped. Her five-year-old son had fled. A search party had hurried together to find him.

Office paperwork had Frank preoccupied. I had no time to fetch him. I jumped on Warrior, and away we flew, leaving a whirlwind of dust behind us. By the time we arrived at Lou's home, the boy had been found hiding in thick brush along the roadside. Three women huddled over a distraught young lady who held her son tightly against her.

Lou told me the young lady's name—Sapphire. I stood rock still, stunned. *So this is Spurger's revenge,* I thought. *This man has no decency. He is evil through and through.*

Lou left to talk with the men outside. I stood in the corner of the room. Sapphire had moved to a chair away from the bed's bloody mess. Time seemed to drag. After what seemed longer than a few minutes, I pulled a chair next to Sapphire's. Through sobs and groans, she told her story.

"Billy-Billy gone to town to git supplies. I was here alone with Noah. I didn't thank nothin' of it 'cause he go to town ever' month to git thangs fer de fawm and de groceries and such ... I was here ironin' ... been ironin for a long while when a man he knock on door. Short ... square ... look like a box ... big aums. I go to door. He push his way inside. 'You all alone; we gonna have fun' he say. I hit him in de head with de hot iron. He staggered back then he pull out knife. He ripped off my dress ... cut off my bra ... put hands all over me. He throw me on bed and push into me ... but when he get started, he don't pay no attention to knife ... I grab it. Cut him on chest an' aums. He bleed all over me, but he grab knife and keep on wit his pleasure ... my boy in bawn here racket an' come to door ... man see him, jump up ... when pullin pants on he stumble over chair ... fall hit head where iron done got him. He groan ... lyin' there. I got his knife off the bed to stab him with. He knock me down an' run after my boy. I run out of the house ... naked with blood all over ... screamin' and yellin' ... I screamed and screamed. Mista Lou heard me screaming for my boy ... Mista Lou come up an' ast me what happen..." Sapphire finally stopped for a breath.

One of the women filled me in on the rest of the story. Lou had ridden quickly to town to find me, while his two oldest sons grabbed their firearms and a couple of butcher knives and a pitchfork and ran back toward Guidry's house hoping to find the boy before the rapist found him. They'd discovered Noah in some brush growing along the road near the farmhouse. They had spotted a man outside the barn, but he fled on horseback.

Frank arrived with our saddlebags and caught up on the story quickly.

"Pack Hardy did it," I told him. "She described him perfectly."

Hanging out of the saddle, Frank began circling the barn in ever-widening spirals until he found tracks of a single horse stretching across the prairie.

"He's got a couple of hours on us, maybe more. We won't catch him tonight."

Chapter 31

WE FOLLOWED THE TRACKS until dusk. We made camp in a bend of a small creek. We tethered our horses close in the open prairie. We were sitting by a campfire watching the sparks fly up as if they were quickening to heaven. The stars seemed so close that I could reach up and pull them into my heart. I was enjoying my whiskey, feeling comfortable and peaceful. Frank had a coffee cup in his hand. We began reflecting on the injuries that we had overcome and our close calls with death.

"I was thinking about what I told you when I was shot by McSween," Frank said. "I had a long recovery—a long, long recovery. I heard the doctor tell the family—all of them were there as much as I could tell—I heard him tell 'em I wasn't going to make it. I was just lying there. Couldn't move. Maybe I was in a coma, but could hear. I don't know ... but when I heard the doc say that ... I heard another voice ... maybe a whisper like ... no more like a thought in my head, but it was coming from somewhere else, somewhere NOT IN MY MIND." Frank raised his voice when he said that. "The thought said something like ... I can't tell you exactly what it said word for word ... but the thought said something like, 'Don't be fearful; don't worry. I am with you and will always be with you. I have some mighty plans for you.' I immediately felt comforted and peaceful. I knew I would live."

Whoa, I said to myself. In all my Methodist circuit riding days, I never heard anything like this.

"Ma & Pa said I was out of it most of the time. That's when the angel came to me, I think. Came several times. Now don't let me talk about religion too long because I got a lot of that Christianity in me."

I couldn't imagine Frank saying something like that. *You really can't know a person's heart*, I said to myself.

"Faith is a tough thing," Frank said. "What did the centurion say to Jesus, 'I believe, help me with my unbelief?' I do know this: Everything God does has a cause behind it. Might take us a long time to recognize it, but there's a cause behind what happens. May not know the cause until we get to heaven, but there's a cause, sure enough. I know this because that angel told me. Probably wouldn't have believed that if the angel hadn't told me."

This sounded like predestination to me. I'm Methodist down to the very last marrow in my bones. Don't like predestination. I believe God gives us free will; otherwise, we'd be like puppets. Can't love a puppet. They're made of wood. I didn't argue the point. I wanted to hear more about Frank's angel.

"Now you might get faith from the Bible if you read it right," Frank said. "You might or you might not. But faith is deep down in your heart all the time. God gives all of us faith. Most people reject it, but a few accept it."

Now that's good Methodist theology I learned at Yale College. *Frank must take that faith thing both the John Calvin way and the John Wesley way*, I thought. Prevenient grace John Wesley called it: the grace that everybody gets: the grace that makes us feel that there is a God; the hound of heaven, the Catholics call it: the feeling that we are missing something. Everybody—from every race, from every culture, from every civilization, from the jungle to the desert—gets that grace call deep in their hearts.

"You most likely won't get it from church," Frank said. "Well maybe some can, but not me. I went to church just about every Sunday with my family. Had to. It was expected of me. I thought it was all a fake ... and I was faking it by going. Didn't want to rile Ma or Pa though, so I kept on going. I got faith when that angel came to visit when I was lying there hardly able to move, not eating much—a little soup, maybe—sipping a little water from time to time."

I put a couple of logs on the campfire, poked at the dying embers. The logs caught, and flames licked toward the sky.

"After I got sort of healthy," Frank said, "I could sit up, drink some water, and eat a little solid food, my heart got heavy, and I didn't know why. But that angel kept visiting when I was sleeping and told me to lighten my heart. The angel sent this thought, 'I must realize my sin and confess it to God ... and be sincere because he knows when you are lying. Then just ask God to forgive you in the name of Jesus Christ and your heart will be right. Your heart will be light.'"

Preach it, Frank; preach it, I thought in my heart ... just like a Baptist in the Amen corner.

"Well I thought and thought about all my sins," Frank said. "No: that's not exactly right. That angel helped point them out to me. Makes me wonder if I'd still be wallowing in sin like a hog in slop if that angel hadn't come by."

"We aren't Puritans," I said. "I sin every day. I worship myself more than I worship God. I focus on my work more than I focus on God. I put my loved ones over God. I try to put God first in my life, but I keep focusing on worldly things. We are human beings. We sin. When we recognize our sins and ask God to forgive us, God will forgive us. When we ask the Holy Spirit to help us live lives that please God, we can begin to live a life worthy of God. The key, I think, is recognizing our sin, asking God for forgiveness, and asking for help to become God centered."

"The angel he showed me. Wait a minute. I'm not sure what that angel was—a he or a she. He was tough as Cooter's goat and as kind as Mother Mary. Anyway, the angel pointed those sins out to me. Cussing at God. Beating up on people just because I could. Disrespecting women. Treating them like things instead of human beings. You know 'slam, bam, thank you ma'am,' like that sort of thing. Thinkin' evil things in my heart ... and pride ... that was the big thing—pride."

"You have a lot to be proud about," I said.

"Maybe so; maybe, not. But pride will take away your soul faster than a boulder pushed over a cliff," Frank said.

I sat there for a while thinking about my pride, looking up at the stars. I took a big gulp of whiskey. I thought about my other sins. *Maybe I haven't been saved yet*, I thought. Wouldn't be the first time a preacher wasn't saved. I took another long sip of whiskey, and my thoughts began to settle down some.

By and by, Frank said, "Don't get me wrong. My heart gets heavy at times. I know I've let Jesus down many a time. But I know this: Faith makes me brave. I can take bullets flying at me and won't flinch. Just keep going until the job is done. I know I won't die until God says I'm ready. When God is ready, I'm ready."

Frank stirred the fire. The moon was shining bright. I got up and walked over to a little hill where I could see the Navasota River winding its serpent-like way through the prairie to where it meets up with the Brazos; near where the Texas Declaration of Independence was signed in 1836, Washington-on-the-Brazos.

We should not have joined the United States in 1845. Things would be better if we were our own country. If we had Texas law, we could get rid of evil monsters the Texas way. I stood there for a long while thinking about what I'd do to Hardy and other rapists—to Spurger and his ilk that treat the colored like they were subhuman. *Maybe I'm not a Christian. Maybe I've been preaching, but not thinking right, not doing right*, I thought.

Presently I heard a wolf howl way down on the prairie somewhere—a long and lonesome howl—and then the whole pack started yapping.

Chapter 32

THE NEXT EVENING AS the sun glittered the western sky with vivid purples, we rode up a hill. Below us, we saw the Colorado River coursing its way out of sandstone bluffs and cliffs and beyond that, on to the rolling prairie where sumac shrubs, elm and willow trees clustered along the river. To our right, woods dense with blackjack and post oaks led down to the river. I got a spyglass out of my saddlebag. I scanned along the river and saw some movement under a cottonwood. I handed the spyglass to Frank. His eyes were much better than mine.

"It's him ... short, square, looks like a box, big arms—just like Sapphire described him. It's Hardy, all right," he said. "We can make our way through those woods down to the river easy enough."

We tethered our horses behind a pomegranate shrub grove. We began picking our way through the woods down to the river. Frank had his Remington Model 8 autoloader. I carried my takedown. We stopped at the edge of the woods and settled down until sundown. We didn't talk. I looked up at the blue sky and watched three buzzards sailing in the soft breeze, looking for their next meal. When light lingered from the set sun, we crept across the flats and along the river as noiselessly as we could. The only sound we heard was the hushed resonance of the river meandering through a sandbank ravine. We moved on slowly through a willow grove. In the moonlight, we could see a sharp bend in the river carving a wide sandbank. Hardy hovered over a small fire.

The tree cover gave out less than 100 yards from the campfire. We walked out in the open. When Hardy saw us, he began running along the sandbank. He was fully exposed. He had nowhere to turn.

Frank called out, "Stop, Hardy."

Almost simultaneously, I yelled, "Hardy, you are only 100 yards away. Hamer can kill you if you are a half-mile away, and he will do it."

I held my hand up to stop Frank who had his Remington aimed toward Hardy. I had seen this stance at target practice many times: his elbows perpendicular to the rifle with the left hand wrapped around the Remington's barrel stem, his right hand behind the trigger wheel and the right index finger over the trigger.

Hardy jogged a few steps. He ran sort of hesitant-like, considering his options.

Frank yelled, "I'll blow your spine right through your heart. On the count of three. One..."

Hardy stopped dead still as if he had run into a brick wall. He put his hands up and slowly turned. His clothes were blood stained, and there were knife slices on his arms.

"Nice and easy now," Frank said in an almost soothing voice, his rifle aimed steady on Hardy's chest as he turned. "Now slow-like. Very deliberately unbuckle your gun belt, and let it slide to the ground. Now your knives. Toss them. Start walking toward us."

Hardy did as commanded. I pressed my cut-down into his lower spine. Huddled close together, the three of us walked back behind some Sumac bushes where Hardy's horse was tethered. Hardy took the reins and began leading his horse. We walked up the hill to our horses. When we got there, I took the reins and tethered them to my saddle horn.

"Mount up," I said as I pointed the shotgun at his chest so he could climb into the saddle. We rode in the bright moonlight with my shotgun pointed at Hardy. No one spoke.

We camped for the night under a limestone outcrop. We ate some jerky and hardtack without a campfire. I left the whiskey in the saddlebag.

"You've tracked me for nothing. No one in Navasota will convict me," Hardy said as he rolled over with his back to me resting his head on his saddle seat.

I took the first watch. Frank wrapped up in his saddle blanket. He began to snore almost immediately. I sat with my back against a limestone overhang, the shotgun across my lap. The moon had set. Millions of stars filled the sky. I felt the warm earth below me, listened to gentle wind blowing through the buffalo grass, and enjoyed the smell of the prairie sages mixed with the scent of wildflowers growing in bunches in the shallows of the rolling prairie. When the big dipper rolled halfway through the sky, I woke Frank. I fell asleep as soon as I folded down in a slight depression amongst the wildflowers.

Chapter 33

I WOKE WITH THE NOISE of Frank building a fire. We drank some cowboy coffee. I had a slab of bacon in my saddlebags. We ate that along with some grits. Hardy sat sullenly. He refused to eat.

I handed the reins to Hardy as he mounted his horse.

"I should have shot you at the river," Frank said. "I hope you try to escape so I can shoot you dead. It will save a lot of time and trouble."

Hardy said nothing. We urged the horses toward Navasota. A building thundercloud rumbled in the east as we rode into town near dark. The saloons were doing a brisk business. No one seemed to notice when we escorted Hardy into the jailhouse. We released a sobered-up drunk and shifted the occupants of the other cells so we could put Hardy in the cell nearest to the office. I closed the door behind him and locked it.

I walked to the Emporium for dinner. I brought back some pork loins and peas on a tin plate.

When I came back, Frank had returned to reading *The Clansman*. He had his feet on the floor and was leaning forward over his office desk. He looked disgusted.

"This book is filled with lies," Frank said. "Dixon wrote *The Clansman* in support of racial segregation. He reverses history. He makes the members of the Klan heroes. The blacks and those who support them are villains.

The blacks are violent savages committing crimes such as murder, rape, and robbery,"

"A lot of people in the South like that book. A lot believe it," I said.

"Correct," Frank said. "The book's white villain, Augustus Stoneman, wants to secure the Southern black vote so the Republican Party would stay in power. He hates President Johnson because Johnson refused to take away the vote of Southern whites. He blames plantation owners for the assassination of Abraham Lincoln. He seeks revenge by stripping away the land owned by whites, giving it to former slaves. Men claiming to represent the government confiscate the material wealth of the South. Former slaves are taught that they are superior to the Southern whites. The blacks pillage the south creating mayhem wherever they go. These injustices are the impetuses for the creation of the Klan."

"It's *Uncle Tom's Cabin* in reverse," I said.

Frank nodded his head in agreement. "There is a character in the book named Gus who rapes a white woman, and murders white men. In Harriet Beecher Stowe's book the benevolent black Uncle Tom is portrayed as angelic."

"Many southerners would burn *Uncle Tom's Cabin* if they had a match," I said.

"People make truth what they want it to be," Frank said. He stood up and put a marker in the book to save his place. "I'm going to Mollie's for dinner," he said. He put on his hat and he walked out the door.

I filled a cup with water. I passed the tin plate of food and the cup of water to Hardy through a small opening in his cell door.

"I want that trial tomorrow so I can get out of this stinking cell," he said.

Chapter 34

THE GRIMES COUNTY Courthouse, situated at the center of the town square, had been erected in 1894. Like almost all 19-century county courthouses in Texas, the edifice presented the most imposing structure in the county. The three-story courthouse had been constructed of hand-molded red brick with limestone details, covered by a steeply pitched roof surmounted by four chimneys and a wood framed cupola with flared eaves. A double-sided staircase on the front of the building rose to the entrance of the district courtroom.

In the early morning, crowds began to gather around the courthouse. At eight o'clock, I unlocked Hardy's cell and cuffed him. I followed him out into the street, my takedown at my side. The crowd parted when we reached the courthouse. I marched Hardy up the right-sided staircase, through the entrance, and down the hall to the courtroom. I sat him down behind a table in front of the judge's bench. I sat on the first row of the gallery directly behind Hardy. I held the pistol handle of my cut down against my right hip and pointed the barrel at the ceiling. Frank took the aisle seat on the back wall of the courtroom. A few minutes later, spectators, mostly men with a few women scattered here and there, packed the courtroom and spilled into the corridors and staircases. The blacks, young and old, men and women, crammed the second story balcony.

Women like Mollie have a way about them. She sat in the middle seat of the front row of the courthouse. Even in a crowded courtroom with pushing and shoving all around, Mollie had, with seeming effortlessness, gained the best seat in the house. The lusterless, dull browns and grays worn by those surrounding her gave a luminescent glow to the white dress and hat she wore. When I saw her, I thought of twilight skies and sparkling fireflies.

Judge Carter, who had been elected by the White Union's votes, opened court at 9:00 AM. The prosecuting attorney, Calvin Hubbard, was Secretary-Treasurer for the local White Man's Union, and a close friend of Robert Spurger. Jeremiah T. Blecher, Spurger's private attorney represented Hardy. Immediately, jury selection began. By 9:45 AM, twelve jurors had been chosen. Hubbard and Blecher, working together, rigged the jury in favor of Hardy. Five of the jurors were associated in some way—carpenters, farriers, suppliers—with Spurger; another, Slim Shaw, was a bootlegger and Ku Klux Klan leader; two tenant farmers and a sharecropper had loans from Brazos Bank owned by Spurger. The other two jurors were low-life drifters, easily swayed by the majority. The outcome had been decided before the trial began.

Calvin Hubbard called his first witness, Sapphire Guidry. Her light black skin had lost its previous luster. She had on an ankle length, full-sleeved white cotton dress. Her bent posture and small shuffling steps reminded me of an old lady. She groaned when sitting in the chair. During the interview, she clasped both hands over her abdomen. Her right eye was swollen shut, her lips were puffed, and there were cuts around her bruised neck.

Through sobs and cries Sapphire's vivid description of the rape seemed to sway the onlookers in her favor. On cross-examination, Blecher confused Sapphire with convoluted questions, attempting to suggest the rapist could have been another man.

Lou Brickman's son, Howard, testified that he had seen Hardy riding away from the barn, but Blecher got Howard to admit that Hardy's presence near the barn failed to prove that Hardy raped Sapphire.

Dr. Coleman testified about Sapphire's extensive injuries. Blecher asked if any of the injuries proved that Hardy raped Sapphire. "So the injuries could have been caused by anyone," Blecher said when excusing Dr. Coleman from the witness stand.

Both Frank and I testified that Hardy had stab wounds on his chest and shoulders, and a large bruise on his head.

After lunch, Blecher called Hardy's common-law-wife, Susie O'Brien, who testified that Hardy had no need to rape Sapphire, as she supplied all his needs. She gave bawdy details that titillated the spectators, but proved nothing.

Spurger testified that Hardy was an outstanding employee who always followed orders. Blecher called three character witnesses. All three seemed to live on the shady side of virtue, but they did a good job extolling Hardy.

As his last witness, Blecher called Hardy to testify in his own defense. After he was sworn in, Hardy stood. "Sapphire Guidry is a bald-faced liar. I didn't rape her. If she was raped, somebody else done it."

Testimony ended at 4:30 PM. Within thirty minutes, the jury declared Hardy not guilty. Hardy swelled his chest like a rooster about to crow. Sapphire sobbed pitifully. Billy-Billy looked as cold and rigid as a corpse. Mollie's head went down as she slumped in her seat. Spurger's deep, brown eyes glowed like smoldering coal, obscuring his pupils. There were a few cheers. Those that clapped partially covered the groans of disbelief from others. A low, mournful burst of grief came from the throng of Negros in the balcony. I trembled with sickening surprise. When I looked back at Frank, he was staring at Hardy with those cold, jump-out-of-the-way snake-like eyes.

Chapter 35

THE SOUTHEAST PORTION of Grimes County, rich with rolling green hills of fertile knee-high grass, made for some of the best ranching in all of Texas. There, John H. Cameron, Mollie's father, had a vast ranch flowing with undulating waves of buffalo grass scattered with grazing Hereford cattle. The ranch extended to Bowie's Creek, deep in the pinewood forest, fenced off against cattle roaming into the tall woods thick with brambles and thorns.

Before he died, Mr. Cameron had dammed up the creeks forming tank ponds for watering cattle and had built barns and a four-cowboy bunkhouse. His rambling home walled with limestone cut in Austin had a wide veranda wrapping around the house from where we could watch the Herefords moving slowly across the landscape.

Every now and then, but not frequent enough as far as I was concerned, Mollie would invite Frank, Mance, and me to enjoy barbecue on the veranda. At these dinners, her brother, Robert B., dressed and acted like a dandy. His hair was greased back. He had a handlebar mustache, wore seersucker suits, a colorful bowtie, starched white shirts, and shoes with spats.

He had a different woman with him every time, but you couldn't tell those women apart. Every one of them had store-blonde hair, red lipstick so bright that it would almost blind you, and lots of gaudy makeup. Each wore low-cut evening dresses that accentuated their overflowing bosoms. They giggled a lot. They seemed about as smart as a drowned turkey.

Each one of them cuddled up to Robert B., squeezed his arms, flitted their eyes, nibbled his ear, and acted like they adored him. They weren't in love with him. They were in lust with him. Lust for his money. Robert B. didn't seem to care as long as he got a couple of long looks down deep cleavage.

Their cooing and clawing embarrassed all of us. We tried to ignore them. After our third dinner, Robert B. and his woman-of-the-month never attended. We supposed that Mollie suggested that they would enjoy deeper intimacy if they ate alone in a restaurant candle-lit for romance.

After that, our dinners were cheerful, thoughtful, filled with love and laughter. We discussed many topics. With the dessert, Mance began playing his guitar, which added loveliness to the evening. Around Mollie, Frank seemed charmed by the richness of life. He enjoyed the freedom and humor he felt when bantering with his feisty Mollie. At the dinners, their conversation might go something like this:

"I think I am going to get a bicycle so I can be like those city women," she'd say.

"Exactly what I was thinking. It will advertise that you are a modern woman. Automobiles are going to be lining the streets with Henry Ford's automated factories spitting them out next year. With automobiles on the streets and bicycles on every corner, there won't be room for horses and wagons. You'd fit right in," he'd say.

By her looks, I could tell Mollie knew Frank enjoyed hearing her spirited ideas. Mollie broadened his view and opinions, giving him an outlook far beyond the Pecos River and west Texas outback. She had a just about as clever a brain as his and certainly could express herself better. He enjoyed the fun her progressive ideas generated, and when he disagreed with them, he did not argue the point with deep conviction. He remained a conservative despite all her modern views. Even when he did not accept them, he absorbed her fresh ideas.

Almost always the conversation would twist into serious talk—Governor Campbell; President Taft; cattle breeding; modern progress threatening the way of life as we knew it; outlaws and bandits and the plight of colored folks.

All of us loved Mance. Songs filled with stories about real people intrigued us. His haunting voice and the way his fingers fluttered over the guitar strings, bringing rhythmic magic and sweet melody to the music, thrilled us. We flat out liked hearing him talk the way he did and were always amazed that a young man could think so deeply about universal questions. We could tell questions about race made Mance deeply uncomfortable initially, but as he gradually learned that our interest was meant to understand and help, not harm, he relaxed. Over time, Mance began to trust us and talked more freely with us.

"The colored—they seem so religious. A lot more enthusiastic about God than us white folks, really. Why do you think that is, Mance?" Mollie asked.

"I don't rightly know, Miss Mollie, but I understand from the talk of my kin and folks that in Africa they knew God was after them. They found him in Texas," Mance said. "God give 'em the hope that heaven promises. That gospel preachin' gives us encouragement; those gospel songs ringin' through the fields, makes that sun sink down a little faster. With the 'ception of you's, the white folks sure enough tell us we ain't got no hope here on this Earth. Now you take the white folks. They most likely put their faith in money and all sorts of earthly things. When things get bad for them, they'll probably be puttin' mo favor in God."

After a pause, Mollie said "Mance, I know that women will get voting rights someday, despite resistance to progress some around this table prefer." She looked at Frank and me and smiled a little impish smile that told us we would come around quicker than we thought. "What do you think Mance? Do you think the Negro will get the right to vote again with the poll tax they just voted through preventing coloreds and poor white folks from voting?"

Mance squirmed a little in his seat before replying, "Nawsuh, ma'am, and it ain't all the poll tax nother. Them big bankers and landowner's and other's that run these towns here got us so whipped down that we's too scare't to vote. Them white people got the same mind. Ever' body gather up thankin' the same thing that we's monkey's or some such, not human like they's are."

"We'll see about that," Frank said. He got up, gave Mollie a light kiss on the cheek, beckoned to me, and we walked out toward our horses without saying another word.

Chapter 36

SUMMERS IN TEXAS last from May until November. From time to time after that, cold weather blows in. On an early February morning, it was Texas cold. Blinding sunshine sparkled the azure sky. An ice-chilling wind howled through leafless trees and rattled around the houses and barns, bringing a haunting melancholy to the prairies. A Texas cold doesn't last long, but when it comes blowing out of the North, it's hunker-down-and-hug time.

It was on that blustery, blinding sunny Texas cold afternoon when Mollie entered the jail office wearing a full-length fox coat. She rushed toward the Franklin stove, put her hands out to warm them, and then turned, her back to the fire. The cold air had given her eyes a diamond sparkle. The warmth of the room blushed her face and gleamed her moist lips ruby red. She removed her coat and held it toward me, exposing a sky-blue wool sweater and black wool riding britches tucked into calf-clinging leather boots. Her smile brought a bluebonnet spring day to a cold winter afternoon.

"Where's Frank?" she asked breathless, almost desperate with anticipation.

"Someone broke into the Kelon place. Frank said he could handle it and told me to stay here in case someone else needed help," I said with an embracing smile.

Her demeanor collapsed. "I was afraid of that. As soon as I read this letter, I rushed over here. I'm afraid something bad is going to happen," she

139

said. "This letter ... it's filled with a terrible premonition; it's a beautiful letter, a wonderful letter in a way, but it's dreadful too." She pulled an envelope out of her coat pocket and unfolded a piece of stationary and read the letter to me.

> My dearest Mollie. The memories of the times spent with you linger lovingly in my mind. My heart forever fills with gratitude for your unending love. When I die, and wanton wind sweeps to dust, the hopes of future years spent with you, my love, will wait for you in eternity. If the dead can flit unseen around those they love, I shall always be near you. A whispered touch upon your cheek shall be my kiss; a soft breeze in the evening air shall be my spirit passing by.

Frank, I didn't know you were such a romantic, I thought.

"I read the letter over and again. It's heart poetry," Mollie said. She paused, looked at me as if she wanted to know if I understood. "But so foreboding."

"Heart poetry—that's a nice phrase," I said. Sometimes when we awaken in the dead of night, we remember blissful times and wish they could last forever. At those times, we contemplate how we can live without those we hold so dear: what it would be like for us without those we love ... and in turn what it would be like for those we leave behind.

Molly had a tender look in her eyes. She didn't say anything.

"I don't think those words are a premonition of death as much as it was Frank trying to express his love for you," I said.

For a moment, we stood there gazing into the fire. "I didn't know he could write so well," Mollie said.

"He reads a lot. Voracious readers usually write well," I said. "Besides, he's been reading Burns, Keats, and Shelly lately. Puts him in a romantic state of mind." I didn't want to say that I thought his words were a little overblown ... but when in love, we tend toward the excess.

"It's awfully sentimental for a Texas Ranger," Molly said.

"The courageous are often romantics," I said. "It takes a fervent heart to fight for the things you deeply believe in."

"This letter ... this letter filled my heart with sweet, melancholy sobs of joy." She looked at me apologetically, wanting to know if she were being too melodramatic.

I smiled. Heart poetry. Sweet, melancholy sobs of joy. *Oh Mollie, you are just as romantic as Frank.*

"I wanted to tell him. I didn't want to telephone him. I wanted to tell him in person how much I love him ... and I wanted to be certain that he was safe. Now that he left without you, I'm even more fearful, no matter what you say."

She paused and looked at me again. I couldn't hold her gaze. I dropped my eyes. Looking into the eyes of someone you love—but who doesn't love you, digs a deep well of melancholy despair.

"Do you think I'm being silly ... worried about him? Being silly to rush over and tell him I love him?"

Did Frank have a premonition? Am I being too cavalier about his letter? I couldn't imagine any outlaw that Frank couldn't handle. Of course, none of us know when we will be gone until the moment we leave. "It's never too early to tell someone you love them," I said.

As soon as I said those words, I realized they were a cliché found in every romance novel. I guess, though, it's not a cliché when said to someone you truly love.

Mollie took a rocker by the Franklin stove. I went out on the porch to fetch some more firewood. When I returned with a full load of cordwood cradled in my arms, Mollie was gently rocking, watching the flickering flames through a crack in the stove door. I put most of the wood in the log rack, opened wide the stove door, and threw in a couple of hickory logs. I turned with my back to the stove.

Just then two young black men flew through the jailhouse door, and Frank walked in behind them. "Caught them down in Hempstead trying to sell the goods they stole," he said.

— • —

Later that night, I became sentimental myself. No. I began feeling sorry for myself. After all, I loved Mollie as fervently as Mollie loved Frank. My loving Mollie was the cruelest of loves because I couldn't tell her how much I loved her. But if Frank could write a letter to Mollie, so could I. So I did:

> When you enter, the room sparkles. All eyes fix on you, the beguiling woman with a powerful can-do spirit fueled by Texas joy. Your vim and vigor transfix all you encounter. When I think of you, I recall a tinkle of laughter, eyes sparkling like diamonds, a convivial smile, and buoyant step; the infectious cadence of a voice; but of all the pleasures I recall the most precious is how deeply you warm my heart when I'm with you.

I read it, and over again. Then I crumpled the page and threw it in the fire.

Chapter 37

By the spring of 1909, the streets were more peaceful. Navasota began to settle down. Gentler times allowed Frank and Mollie to enjoy more hours together. During the full flush of bluebonnet season, Frank and Mollie married at the Cameron mansion to much fanfare. The aristocratic families attended along with the town's movers and shakers. Robert B., in charge of the gala, outdid himself. At the reception, butlers in white coats served drinks on the Saint Augustine lawn. The scrumptious buffet had every delicacy imagined. Mance entertained the crowd. No one objected.

There was no more lynching after Frank and I came to town. Of course, racial tensions still existed. On one such occasion, a 10-year-old boy hit a colored boy over the head with a rock. The father of the black boy stabbed the father of the white boy three times. The black man was sentenced to serve 15 years in the Huntsville State Prison. While waiting for transfer to Huntsville, the man spent several days in the Navasota jail. Frank and I took turns guarding the jail. No mob attempted to break into the jail, drag the man out, and hang him. Attacks on blacks became rare. When they did occur, the offending man would spend a week or more in a jail cell.

Underneath the aura of peace, Spurger seethed. His diminished power and control enraged him. He went to the Allen Farm more often than in the past. Mance told us he took his anger out on the help, beating and whipping them. Our visits to Allen Farm failed to curtail his fury. Mildred told us that Spurger had increased clandestine meetings with those who had profited from a wide-open town, but she could tell us nothing specific about his plans.

Mance continued to drive the buggy, carrying me out to the plantations to encourage better treatment of the colored help. The plantation patrols that we took seemed to have some effect on diminishing abuse of the black workers. When we were on the plantation, everything appeared peaceful, but Mance told me that when we left, the blacks were treated roughly again.

There is just so much the law can do. The law cannot suppress all crime. Law certainly cannot stop sin. Any law that attempts to legislate morality will not work. No law will prevent prostitution from flourishing. Laws against wagering simply drive gambling underground. Trying to regulate liquor increases crime. Legal injunctions against drugs engender smuggling. Only a change of heart can stop wicked ways.

Most of the business owners were well pleased with the peace that settled over the town. Legitimate businesses boomed as never before.

Mollie's adventurous spirit enamored Frank. He was filled with warm Texas pride when he and Mollie drove up in a wagon that was loaded with a 14-foot alligator. When he pulled the canvas cover off the beast, people began to gather. They came out of saloons, offices, and houses. It seemed as if the entire town's people craned their necks to see the leviathan.

"Mollie shot him three times," Frank bragged. "Bang! Right eye. Bang! Left eye. Bang! Between the eyes. Of course, the right eyeshot got him. The other two shots were just target practice."

"That thang is biggest I ever saw, and I grew up in the Louisiana on the Bayou Teche in Louisiana," one of the town drunks said. "If that thang in my dreams don't stop my drinking, my hen-peckin' wife sure won't."

"I ain't swimming in the Navasot' no more," a schoolboy said.

"Look at the teeth on that monster. He'd saw you in half right quick," a farmer said.

"And eat your sow pig and all her littl'uns," a man in coveralls and a worn-out straw hat said.

"She a better shot than you, Marshal?" Jimmy Lee called out with an impish grin.

"Let's put it this way. If she gets angry with me, I'm not staying around to find out," Frank said with proud eyes and a warm chuckle.

Chapter 38

I MISSED STARDUST. I dreamed of her. Thoughts of the night I spent with her haunted my daydreams. At the same time, my love for Mollie continued to burn. My rage for Hardy smoldered. Things of the world seemed more important than my devotion to God. I read the Bible daily. I prayed. But God was not first in my heart. I craved the love of a woman. I wanted someone to love and someone to love me in return. I began drinking more.

Night had fallen. Peace settled over the streets. Jimmie Lee's Saloon bustled with noise and laughter. Mollie had taken Mance to Dallas to hear Blind Lemon Jefferson sing and play on Deep Ellum Street. Frank stood next to the birdcage teaching the macaw to count to ten in Spanish. Jack Daniel's fogged my thoughts as I leaned against the bar.

Hardy swaggered into Jimmie Lee's Saloon. I hadn't seen him since the trial. How long had he been gone? Six months? Maybe more. He slithered next to me. "Hello, nigger lover," he said.

I almost took a swing at him, but I held back. Hardy took a bandana off his neck. Slowly, methodically, he wiped his face. He put the wet bandana in his back left pocket and pulled his long knife out of the sheath tied to his leg.

"This knife has been covered with some mighty sweet blood," he said.

Before I could react, Frank leaped toward Hardy and gave him a swirling roundhouse kick in the head. Hardy crumpled onto the floor, unconscious.

Frank grabbed Hardy by the scruff of the shirt and pulled him over to the brick wall. He pounded Hardy's head into the wall—one, two, three times. Frank let go of Hardy's shirt, and the punk thudded onto the saloon floor like a sack of flour.

A death-like stillness surrounded the room. Then subdued sobs came from a few women. The men seemed petrified. Everyone stared at Frank with horrified looks on their faces. They had never seen such fury. Neither had I. Frank turned toward the crowd, his eyes burning with rage. The ferocious intensity of his gaze caused those nearest him to stumble backward.

"Trans Pecos law," Frank said.

Hardy lay on the floor unconscious. He emitted a rasping, gurgling sound with each breath. Someone left hurriedly and soon returned with Dr. Coleman. Leonard got on his knees to examine Hardy. He listened to his chest. He peered into the thug's eyes. He tapped Hardy's knees with a rubber hammer he had pulled out of his coat. He took the man's boots off and ran the tapered shaft of the rubber hammer up the bottom of each foot.

"I think this man will live, but they'll be spoon feeding him the rest of his life if he does," Dr. Coleman said.

Chapter 39

BY LATE MAY, bluebonnets that had colored the prairies had been replaced by multicolored wildflowers. The trees were in full leaf and the landscape a lush green. The temperate weather gave promise of a cool summer, a promise never kept. Mance and I drove into town on the buggy after inspecting the Allen Farm. Everything had looked peaceful.

I cleaned up and headed for Jimmy Lee's Saloon. I was sipping a whiskey and reading the *Navasota Examiner-Review*. Frank was teaching Sir Isaac Newton to say treachery when lo and behold, our old pal Monty Motes walked in. He had a shiny Texas Ranger badge pinned over his left vest pocket. Frank and I erupted with whoops and cheers.

"Say 'howdy' to the bona fide and certified Texas Ranger Monty Motes," Frank told Newton as he turned with a wide grin on his face and extended his hand. "I see Captain Rogers took the word of ole' Judge Roy Bean and signed you up."

I was surprised when Frank ordered a whiskey. I ordered Jack Daniel's for Monty and me. He didn't demure. This was celebration time. No Dr. Pepper for him. We clinked our glasses together. The three of us sat at our usual table, giving a clear view of the street.

"It's been over a year. We've been reading about your heroics in the papers," I said excited to see our friend.

"Captain Rogers wrote that you have gained his trust. He's been sending you on some of the toughest assignments in Texas. Tell us about it," Frank said with eagerness in his voice.

Monty leaned forward in his chair. He seemed distracted, almost somber. Not the Monty we had met on the train. "My first assignment was the Sherman debacle, but I arrived a day late. By that time, the mob had burned down the courthouse, taken the poor African's roasted body out of the vault safe, hung him from a Sycamore, and started another fire under the body. When I got there, I had nothing to do but cut the body down and arrange for a burial. I wanted to shoot every darn one of the mobsters, but after the mob has done their thing, there is no one to shoot."

Monty's restrained descriptions gave the facts without the glorified details that we had heard on our long train ride from Langtry to Austin.

"After that, they sent me to Fort Worth to deal with some bankers who were giving bounty for the dead body of any bank robber. I discovered that some thugs had staged the robberies to collect the bounty money. They pay a retard $100 to break a window and steal whatever money he could find in bank drawers. The next day, they would shoot him and bring the body and the stolen money to the bank commissioners, who would then give the gang a $5000 reward. It was mighty satisfying getting that gang behind bars."

He's different, I thought. Not exuberant. Not gregarious. All law and order as in the past, but without the enthusiasm.

"In the Slocum massacre, 200-300 whites got into a fight with a Negro settlement on the east side of town. They killed 200 blacks. A few, very few were able to escape and fled to Tyler. Their little community was burned to the ground. I investigated. No one in the entire town knew anything. When I asked about ashes and two or three burned lean-tos that once could have been a house, no one knew anything about a fire."

"People up that way aren't known for their brilliance," I said with sarcasm in my voice.

We told Monty about the challenges we had faced, but the camaraderie that the three of us once had for each other seemed missing. An unseen force percolated through the room, disrupting a free-spirited harmony.

Suddenly, conversation ceased. We sat there, the three of us, looking at our empty shot glasses. No one spoke. I couldn't think of anything to say. I twisted in my seat and looked out the window. I felt a disturbing sense that something was wrong. An empty, nervous feeling swirled in my gut as if I was waiting for a doctor to give me bad news.

Monty looked downhearted. He cleared his throat. His eyes became moist.

"You both know that Pack Hardy died almost three months ago. He never recovered consciousness from the beating you gave him, Frank." Monty paused and looked down for a good bit. No one said anything. Then Monty looked up. He fixed his eyes on Frank. "I was sent here to arrest you Frank."

Frank sat upright, looking at Monty with warmth in his eyes. It seemed to me that Frank's empathy for Monty's terrible assignment concerned him more than the future he faced.

"Robert Spurger wrote Captain Rogers about Pack Hardy. He wrote another letter to Governor Campbell," Monty said. "Governor Campbell and the Captain met. They decided to deep six the case because of your outstanding record and all the good you had done for Texas. Spurger then began writing state legislators. He even wrote a letter to United States Senator Charles Allen Culberson. Governor Campbell capitulated."

Monty paused. I squirmed in my seat. Frank looked completely relaxed as if he were sitting on the banks of a spring-fed creek, fishing.

Monty looked gloomy. "Since you are the law around here, there is no one to arrest you. They sent me." Monty looked around the saloon. His eyes rested briefly on the macaw. He turned his eyes back to Frank. "You are under arrest, Frank. Let's head for the jail."

The three of us got up and headed for the Saloon's swinging doors. I trailed a few steps behind the others. Malice and loathing toward Spurger filled my heart. A venom taste filled my mouth. As I passed through the doors, Newton squawked "treachery."

Chapter 40

THE SUN'S SLOW DESCENT in the late afternoon sky did little to reduce the blistering heat we had suffered that windless summer afternoon. Monty, Mollie, and I used handheld funeral fans to cool ourselves as we sat outside the bars of Frank's cell. The oppressive heat amplified our despondency.

I had jailed many men destined for the gallows. Some raged with ceaseless expletives. Others cried pitilessly. Many denied their guilt. Two felt certain of rescue. One man rolled over in his bunk with his face to the wall and slept until the hangman appeared. One or two called for a priest; another asked for baptism. Unremitting, hideous, and dreadful terror flooded the hearts of many.

Frank talked. "I understand that when decent people know death approaches, they wish they had spent more time enjoying the simple pleasures of life, and they regret spending so much time fretting over little things and working for worldly treasures.

"Not me. What's done is done. I enjoy looking back at the adventures—gun fights, drunken brawls, bawdy women; when I've laughed and what I've learned. My love for you—Mollie ... a treasure, diamonds, rubies, pearls. Our friendship, Jude ... like a brother, brother. Huckleberry Monte—the law and order man, Charlie Goodnight's man.

"I'm not a look-back guy. I'm a look-forward man. My remorse comes from the things undone. I've got a lot of things to do. I've got a lot of people to love. I've got a lot of evil to defeat ... and I'm concerned I will get bored in heaven. I'm not big on pearly gates, streets of gold, and angel harps. I don't want to be sitting around polishing my halo.

"Heaven. That's an interesting subject. Heaven is right here; right now. We just can't see it with our temporal eyes. We fix our eyes on things that are seen. We don't notice the eternal things that are right here with us this very moment. The kingdom of God is within. The Holy Spirit offers guidance each and every minute. The love of God surrounds us. Jesus dwells amongst us. When I focus on Jesus, I feel him hovering over my right shoulder. God has flooded our world with beauty. Love surrounds us. We just have to look for it."

— • —

The four of us heard a horse gallop to a stop outside the jailhouse. The door opened. A dusty rider handed me an official looking document. Governor Campbell had declared a change of venue. No Spurger-led kangaroo court for Frank. A fair trial in Austin gave a better chance for acquittal. The news spread quickly. Mildred told us that the declaration enraged Spurger. When he heard the report, Spurger hurled a whiskey bottle across the bar counter, shattering the gilded mirror at Throop's saloon.

I was thrilled. I looked around. Monty and I sat on the jailhouse porch. I had dozed off, dreaming.

Chapter 41

THE NOOSE HAD NOT coiled yet. The trail date had been set for Monday at the Grimes County Courthouse. A change of venue was possible. Peter Welsh Shine had taken the train to Austin. He had an appointment with Governor Campbell. There was an awfully good chance that the Governor could be persuaded to move the trial to Austin. I wondered if Spurger might be thinking the same thing. If so, what would be his plan?

I discussed this possibility with Monty. We both agreed that Spurger would strike if Governor Campbell ordered a change of venue.

"In the meantime," Monty said, "Frank remains in this jail. It's the law."

Frank was locked in the first cell nearest the door. The last time I had looked in on him, he had been reading Dixon's newest book, *The Traitor*.

"More Dixon?" I asked.

"Still trying to understand how racists think," he replied. He seemed indifferent to the impending trial.

"We're all racist. You don't seem to value Mexicans. I hate Arabs," I said.

"Where have you met an Arab? I don't think Texas has any," Frank said.

"Read about them. They make their women wear Burkas in public to protect their purity while screwing a whole harem of naked virgins," I said.

"You're just jealous," Frank said.

We sat there for a while, lost in our own thoughts. I decided I was being too cavalier about this racist thing. Finally, I said, "I guess we are all biased. The Muslims hate the Jews: the Russians hate the Serbs; the Germans hate the Poles; the Irish hate the English. The French ... well ... the French hate everybody."

"The whites hate the blacks," Frank said. "I thought I ... we ... could change it. I thought we could protect the blacks—rid the town of black hatred. But we've done nothing. My quest has failed."

"There haven't been any black hangings since we got here," I said. "And the blacks seem better treated on the plantations."

"That's only when we ride out to check the situation. As soon as we leave, the big boss men and the gun-bulls take over again. We have done nothing to stop this ... what would you call it ... this white supremacy sort of thing. Spurger still lives. When he dies, someone else will come along just as evil. Mance is right. There will be no end to this mistreatment."

"A spiritual revival may help," I said.

"It will take a hell of a spiritual revival. The second coming maybe."

"What about education? I mean, if people knew how badly the blacks were treated wouldn't this knowledge help change attitudes?"

"The ignorant will always be with us," Frank said.

"The law?" I said.

"We *were* the law. What good did we do?" Frank asked. "And some of the most evil people wear badges. They use their authority to suppress others. Besides, you can't legislate morality"

"This entire conversation depresses me. You make it seem so hopeless. This isn't like you, Frank. You are a can-do man. A take-charge man."

"Being locked behind bars tends to suppress action."

"Yes, and I guess sitting around with nothing to do brings on the worst kind of thinking."

"Our thoughts can make heaven a hell or hell a heaven. Imprisonment accentuates the hellish."

"No matter how you are thinking now, your influence has made a positive difference. We all make mistakes. We all have flaws. None of us can change the world, but our behavior—good or bad—can influence those around us. Your decency has made an impact on others. Those you have treated fairly will tend to treat others with respect. And so it goes. Little ripples can turn into big waves."

Frank got up off his cot. He walked to a tiny window in his cell. Outside, the sun shone brightly. A few white, fluffy clouds drifted slowly across the azure sky. We could hear people talking, laughing; children playing; the clip-clop of horses' hooves. Frank's cell seemed to shrink. I wanted to get up, go outside, and breathe the air of freedom, but instead, I sat thinking about what it would be like if I couldn't walk out the door.

"I don't think they will convict me. Hardy deserved to die. I did Texas a favor," Frank replied with a shrug.

Why is Frank so unconcerned, I wondered. Had Frank forgotten how Spurger controlled the Navasota courts? *Doesn't Frank realize Navasota law differs from the law west of the Pecos, ruled with an eye-for-an-eye justice?* Hardy raped a woman. Frank knocked Hardy dead. That's justice according to Judge Roy Bean.

"Besides," Frank said interrupting my reverie, "when the Lord decides my time has come, I'm ready. This hanging may be my early ticket to heaven."

"I don't like your Presbyterian way of thinking."

"Couldn't be a Presbyterian. I smile too much."

"And you're not stingy enough. Those Presbyterians are all cookie jar rich. Got all that money stored away."

We sat there for a while. Frank became serious. "The possibility of hanging surely does make me think. Have I been pleasing to God in every way? No. Have I lived a life worthy of the Lord? Sometimes. Have I been fruitful? There is so much more I could have done. At times I've been as lazy as a hound dog on a hot August day. No, I haven't done as much as I

could to help others. I could have done so much more to help the blacks....
That grieves me."

"None of us can do anything to deserve the grace that Jesus offers. His grace has saved you from the dominion of darkness."

"Yes. Thank God for showing us the kingdom of light," he said.

Chapter 42

A FULL MOON WAS RISING. The round, orange globe seemed to fill the eastern sky. Frank got up and walked to his cell window. The moon's light gave him a radiant glow.

Frank stood by the window a long time. "These bars ... they make me realize how precious freedom is."

Frank returned to his bunk. I pulled up a chair. We sat there for a long time.

"I will do everything I can to prevent a kangaroo court," I said.

I hoped Frank didn't hear the despondence in my voice. I didn't know what else to say. So I tipped my hat, turned, and left. What could I do? I couldn't let my best friend hang. I had to break him out. But how? Spurger had his men taking shifts watching the jail. And what about Monty? He was Texas Ranger proud. He saw no bend in the law. He was a Charlie Goodnight man. Law and Order. He would resolutely defend Frank's right for a fair and just trial, but he wouldn't help him escape.

I joined Monty on the porch. We watched the golden glow of the moon slowly rise. For the first time since we'd met, Monty said nothing. They say that when one gets older, time seems to fly by at locomotive speed. Not for us. We were young. Time seemed to creep. By and by, a black cloud settled over the town, obscuring the moon and the stars.

Then, as if awakened from a peaceful dream, I noticed a death-like stillness all around. No piano playing, no laughter, no shouting came from the saloons. The streets had emptied. The clip-clop of horse hooves, the creaking of wagons, footfalls on the slat boardwalks—a sinister silence had replaced the clamor of voices.

I glanced at Monty who, like me, seemed haunted by the spectral hush. Suddenly, as if pushed by a shadowy presence, we both leapt from our chairs. We heard a disturbing murmur. Something was headed toward us. I grabbed for my takedown. Monty rushed inside to snatch the 15-gauge from the gun rack. At the same time, we both realized what was coming. And sure enough, here it came: Shadowy figures smoldering in torchlight and the blood-curdling bellow and boom of mob voices as the rabble pressed spasmodically toward us.

As the mob grew nearer, I could make out individual faces. I saw no Africans, no sharecroppers, no dairy farmers. I recognized the faces of the Spurger's minions—his supporters, the gun-bulls, the goons, and those indebted to him. As the mob surged forward, the individual faces seemed to fuse together into a single-faced horde. Spurger, with a torch held high in his right hand and a rope wound over his left shoulder, led the rabble, stirring the dehumanized mass into a frenzy with his demonic howls: "Hang 'em. Hang the murderer."

When a mob forms, where are the victim's supporters? I thought.

"He will hang Monday at noon. Bring your family. Have a picnic; eat some ice cream as you watch him dangle," Monty shouted above the roar.

"A lawless lawman deserves more than a simple hanging," Spurger howled. "He has a beating coming—a terrifying beating before he hangs."

"No lawman can bang a man's head against a wall, leaving him sure to die," a big man shouted.

The crowd surged closer.

"We'll string him up, burn him with our torchlights as he strangles," Landis cried out.

"Cut him down. Drag him through the streets," someone I couldn't see hollered.

The crowd pushed forward. Yells and shouts from the mob drowned out the Ka-Chung of my shotgun when I racked it. I put it to my shoulder and aimed into the middle of the crowd, but to my astonishment, the mob kept surging forward. The frenetic frenzy of the whiskey-fueled mob fired to fury by just a few rabble-rousers caused day-by-day common folk to lose all sense of reality. At that short distance, one blast from my cut down would send a half-dozen good citizens to hell or Stillwater. I hesitated.

Spurger was a step ahead of the mob, shouting; holding his torch high; waving it forward. He was prodding them; emboldening them; goading them. Spurger surged forward. A few more steps and he would be on the porch, the mob crowding behind.

I raised my shotgun and pointed the barrel directly toward Spurger's chest. Once again, I saw that incredibly contemptuous grin of utter hostile malevolence. In what could be no more than a flash of time, I had a feeling of deep despair. My entire body seemed extraordinarily heavy. I shook off my torpor and shot Spurger full in the chest.

He seemed to crumble but immediately took on a ghastly appearance. He thrashed and twisted like a huge writhing snake of great strength. His eyes sparked red flames of blazing hatred. Fang-like teeth made a hideous grinding sound when he opened and closed his mouth, trying to bite me.

Fear paralyzed me. With great effort, I pumped the shotgun. Ka-Chung. I shot this writhing figure full in the head. Brain, blood, and bone chips splattered the crowd. The ghastly apparition disappeared, and Spurger crumpled to the ground dead.

A mist of a black cloud left the body and hovered over the crowd. The mist settled over Landis, the big boss man. The black vapor coiled around Landis and faded away.

I shook my head. *Shadows from the torchlights fueled my imagination*, I thought. Times of great distress can confuse the mind.

For a beat, time stopped. A sudden hush fell over the crowd. Almost before the echo of the gun blast had died away, a powerful KA-BOOM filled the air. Just beyond the train depot, in the direction of the freight warehouses, tremendous tongues of red, blue, and yellow flame licked high into the dark of night.

Someone yelled, "The armory!"

Booms and blasts filled the air. The mob scattered, propelled toward the flame, running to do what they could to snuff out and beat down the lashing flames before other warehouses became engulfed.

Out of the flames, smoke, and soot all around her, Mollie came flying on her silver stallion Stampede. She held the reins of Bugler galloping close behind. In seconds, she leaped on the porch and opened her right hand toward me, gesturing for the jail keys.

Monty held his Colt by his side. He brought his hand and arm up until his forearm became perpendicular to his chest. Five feet from me, he pointed the massive gun at my torso. He pulled the hammer back; held the pistol steady: "The mob's gone. Frank will have a fair trial," he said.

I locked eyes with Monty. No one moved. No one said anything. For what seemed a long interval, but was probably only a few seconds, Monty held the Colt pointed steadfastly at my chest. Then, with a shrug and a sheepish smile, he carefully released the hammer of the Colt and holstered it. He reminded me of a little boy listening to Charlie Goodnight weave stories of cattle drives long ago. He stepped back. I tossed the keys to Mollie who ran upstairs to unlock the cell door.

Within seconds, they mounted their horses. Frank tipped his hat toward us, and they were gone. The two people I loved most disappeared in the night. I gazed westward into a cloud-dimmed night, hoping for a last glimpse of the unseen riders, obscured by the light of leaping flames to the north of me. I remained there listening to the thunder of hoof beats until a soft breeze blowing across the undulating prairie carried the sounds away. I looked at dark nothingness for a long time: thinking; remembering; wondering. I turned.

Monty stood there, hat in hand, a reverential look on his face. "Texas law sure is iffy at times," he said.

Acknowledgements

In this journey, I have found that writing a book is much like rearing children: it takes a village. I am so thankful for the many people who took the time to read my book, encourage me, and offer suggestions to make it better. Greg and Wende Whitus, Cornel Walker, Tim and Betsy Covington, Bob Smith, Sandy Young, Mark Broomell, Patrick Robinson, and Mike Cavil—your input was priceless. My deepest appreciation goes to my agent Lori Whitus. Without your help, this novel would have never come to fruition. I would also like to thank my editor Kimberly Coghlan. Thank you for working your manuscript magic.

Made in the USA
Columbia, SC
30 January 2023

11224386R00105